THE MAGIC OF KINDNESS

A Novel in Short Stories

Brian Allan Skinner

Nighthawk Press

TAOS, NEW MEXICO

Nighthawk Press
PO Box 1222
Taos, New Mexico 87571
www.nighthawkpress.com

Book Layout & Design by Brian Allan Skinner
Cover art: "A Quilt of Earth & Sky #4" © 2019 by Brian Allan Skinner
All interior illustrations © 2019 by Brian Allan Skinner
www.brianskinner.net

Publisher's Note: This is a work of fiction. Names, characters, places, and incidents are a product of the author's imagination. Locales and public names are sometimes used for atmospheric purposes. Any resemblance to actual people, living or dead, or to businesses, companies, events, institutions, or locales is completely coincidental

The Magic of Kindness / Brian Allan Skinner – 1st edition
ISBN 978-0-9986807-9-8
Library of Congress Control Number: 2019938087

CONTENTS

ACKNOWLEDGMENTS

I want to thank my readers whose generous remarks and five-star reviews provided me so much encouragement. It is, after all, the reassurances of my readers that inspire me to write more tales. It helps to have fans.

My thanks extend to the many reviewers of *Shoot Me, Jesus: Tales of the Old & New Southwest* who took the time to leave their thoughts about my book on Amazon and other venues. Particular thanks go to Johanna DeBiase and Phaedra Greenwood whose glowing reviews and positive appraisals appeared in print.

I also wish to thank my publisher, Rebecca Lenzini of Nighthawk Press, for standing by me despite the less than stellar sales of my previous collection.

The stories in the present volume would not be in anywhere near as good shape without the honest assessments of writers Dianne Vona and Sandra Richardson of the Peerless Critique workshops. Meeting nearly every week at SOMOS, the Society of the Muse of the Southwest, the literary organization of Taos, New Mexico, we discuss each other's work in depth.

One reader I cannot fail to mention for his helpful idea is Henry Morrison. "I wouldn't mind reading another José story," he told me. But I don't like to promise anything. My muse does not always accept my own ideas. But she likes José and thought Hank had a good suggestion, leading to the story "My Two Papas," included in this anthology.

Lastly, but first in my mind, I thank my mother, Elaine, who read to me ceaselessly when I was a child, and to my father, George, who worked overtime at a job he didn't like to afford sending me to a good school. Though both are dead, they live on in me and in my stories.

Brian Allan Skinner

AUTHOR'S NOTE

As with my previous collection of tales, *The Magic of Kindness* is a "novel in short stories." The eight tales in the present volume are connected not only by plot elements, but also by characters who appear in several of the stories.

I draw once again upon my stable of six trustworthy players. Though some of them have changed their names and others wear disguises, no doubt they will still be familiar to you. The personalities of the characters remain somewhat malleable, yet their identities are consistent. They develop by a process of accretion, gradually accumulating traits.

At times I feel I'm merely taking dictation from my characters. But it is their stories I'm telling, after all—not my own.

While I conceived each of these stories as a stand-alone work of short fiction that can be read in any order, the way in which I have presented them is meant to help the reader come to an understanding of who my characters are and what they are about.

Since the publication of *Shoot Me, Jesus*, my previous anthology of stories, I have been encouraged and often inspired by the comments of my readers. It is apparent that they understand what I am trying to accomplish with my connected short fiction. My fellow writers and even my creative writing students have also contributed their suggestions to the work at hand. Daily life provides it own sparks and flashes of insight, too. I may write alone, but the inspiration is a community affair.

The comment I heard most often about my work, after "quirky," was that I have an attentive ear for dialogue. It got me thinking about where I got my ability to hear my characters in their own voices.

While I was permitted as a child to join the company of adults, I was not encouraged to take part in their conversations unless I had been addressed, in other words, to be "seen and not heard." I believe I picked up on the rhythm of conversation, the music of words, long before I understood their meanings or implications. It is upon this framework, like a musical staff, that I hang my characters' dialogue.

Also, in a city as rich in vocal textures and languages as New York City, where I lived for twenty years, dialogue was everywhere in the air. Mere snippets of dialogue from strangers have given rise to many of my stories—more than I would ever be able to tell.

I never hid behind headphones or earbuds, either, enjoying the city at uncensored full volume. Preferring to pay attention to the rich world around me, I was never enthralled by the tiny world on a tiny screen.

Once again I hope you enjoy this collection of tales. Please take a moment to share your comments with me and other readers, either on my Amazon author's page or through my website at www.brianskinner.net. I look forward to hearing from you.

Brian Allan Skinner

THE GIFT

Maxim struggles with the locks of the sixth floor Washington Heights apartment he shares with his mother, sister, and grandmother. Nineteen-year-old Nina and Grandma share the single bedroom. Mama, who works nights at the phone company office way down on Sixth Avenue, has a gold-and-white brocaded sleeper sofa in the living room.

Maxim is a classically-trained pianist who studied at the Odessa Institute in Russia. He and his restored Steinway A grand piano occupy what would have been the dining room, closed off from the kitchen and living room by hideous flowered curtains from Woolworth's that don't quite reach the floor. He calls out before opening the front door all the way.

No one responds except Anastasia, his Grandma's pampered cat. Maxim's mother has left for work and Nina is not yet home from school. Grandma is likely elbowing her way along 181st Street in pursuit of fabric remnants and kitschy bargains.

Maxim kicks off his polished black shoes and nudges them onto the mat inside the apartment door. It is, after all, his mother's bedroom. He removes his tie and rumpled suit jacket before reaching his "piano room." He puts his shirt and jacket on hangers and hooks them onto the window handles. Then he ties the curtains in knots and throws the windows wide open. He stands admiring the view while stripping out of his white undershirt and black trousers.

One window faces south, deeper into Manhattan, and the

other looks west across the Hudson River and the George Washington Bridge. The breeze is strong. He drapes his sweaty undershirt and black socks on the window sills, securing them with heavy picture books on music and musicians. Only two blocks from the highest natural point on the island, Maxim's solid early Twentieth Century apartment building is never without ventilation. He often has to hold the pages of his scores with big metal clips. The building was erected the same year his Steinway was built—1907.

Maxim closes the curtains to his room and fetches the handkerchief from his jacket pocket. He removes his black-framed glasses, cleans the lenses, and wipes his forehead. Then he slides onto the piano bench in just his white boxer shorts. Anastasia pokes her nose beneath the curtains and Maxim pounds out a discordant chord. The cat turns around and sashays off, her raised tail ruffling the curtains.

Though the family came by boat, Grandma paid a lot of money to have the sourpuss feline shipped by air from the USSR when they left Odessa for New York. That had been four years ago, when the Motherland became Russia again and the Soviet Union broke into rusty pieces. Maxim's father, Cyril, had not traveled with them. He'd likely be an old man before he was released from prison.

Maxim stares at the ugly patches in the plaster and wishes he had one of his father's paintings of the Odessa Gardens to hide the cracks and remind him of home. His father's foremost problem had been that he refused to paint in the officially sanctioned style. Cyril Andreyevich also managed to squander the advances on the few commissions he got—usually from block-headed commissars—on vodka and women, in what proportion Maxim never knew. His father never made a single deadline and was nevertheless in demand because his work recalled the old Russia.

Reaching for the score of Rachmaninov's *Etudes Tableaux* that he'd worked on that morning, Maxim closes his eyes. He misses his father. He feels surrounded by bossy women who will never let him live his own life. But he is not likely to see his father for a long time. He'd counterfeited currency for the *Bez Nazvaniya*, the

Not Named. He was a gifted artist who had no talent for making money except as a counterfeiter. Maxim had sent him letters and sketch pads and charcoals. He wonders whether any of them reached his father. Maxim never received a single reply.

"Knock, knock," Nina shouts from the other side of the kitchen curtains forming the other "wall" of Maxim's piano room.

"I'm practicing," he tells his sister. "Why are you shouting? I'm not deaf."

"You didn't answer the first time. I didn't hear any practicing going on. Can I come in?" she asks, her hand already reaching for the curtains.

"I suppose," Maxim says. "But I'd better be making some noise when Grandma gets home."

"I'll keep watch," Nina says. "Grandma always goes the same way, like a wind-up toy."

Nina folds Maxim's now dry undershirt and sets it beside him on the piano bench. She knows better than to touch his Steinway with anything other than a polishing cloth. Glancing down at the knotted strands of traffic and pedestrians on the western end of 181st Street, she pushes the picture books on music aside and sits down on the deep window sill.

"When do you get the headshots, Max? I'm excited to see them. The talent agents will flock to you, I'm sure."

"The photographer lives here in the Heights, so maybe I'll get them tonight if the lab processes the film in time."

"That's nice of him to drop them off to you."

"Her," Maxim corrects his sister. "Her name is Miss Phaedre McGuirk."

"Only in America. What kind of name is that?"

"Her family's Irish. She's very smart about photography. And quite pretty."

"Ah-hah," Nina remarks, raising her eyebrows.

She and Maxim look very much alike: light brown hair and blue eyes. Though she is five years younger than her brother, she has been completely Americanized in Maxim's opinion.

"Here comes Grandma with two big shopping bags. Better get your pants on, Max."

He does not care for the nickname but has given up trying to get Nina to call him by his proper name. He scrambles for his socks and sneakers and a pair of blue jeans. Most of his casual clothes reside in cardboard boxes stacked in the corner. Maxim slips into the white undershirt on the piano bench and draws open all the curtains to the piano room.

"You look like a nerd, Max. Nobody wears black socks with white sneakers except *eem-mee-grants* just off the boat," she tells him, imitating a bad Russian accent.

"Well, what are we? Have you forgotten so soon, Nina?" he reminds her, flipping randomly to a page in the score and plunging right in.

The front door bangs open and Grandma, dropping her shopping bags, plops down onto a brocaded chair by the living room window. She huffs and puffs and fans herself with a Russian newspaper. Grandma is the only old person Maxim and Nina know who recalls the Old Days of the Soviet Union longingly. Her braided gray hair is tucked beneath her babushka.

"It's as hot as the devil's poker out there," she remarks. "Bring your Grandma something cool, and a little something on the side."

Nina brings her a tall tumbler of ice water and a small glass with a double shot of vodka.

"So, continue playing, Maxim. Did the photo kill go well today?"

"It's a photo shoot, Grandma."

"Well, when you shoot somebody, don't you try to kill them?"

Nina rolls her eyes and Maxim lets out a chuckle. Nina unpacks Grandma's parcels. There are two oversized pillows for the sofa in a nearly matching, nearly hideous white-and-gold brocade. At the bottom of each bag is a dead chicken, its plumage intact.

"A man on the *Metró* tells me, 'Lady, you can't come on the subway with live chickens.' So I fix that. *Snap. Snap.* No more live chickens. OK, mister?"

This time Maxim rolls his eyes and Nina laughs. Grandma

takes another swallow of ice water and downs the rest of the vodka.

"OK. You can continue playing, Maxim," she tells her grandson.

He picks up precisely where he left off. Grandma leans back in the easy chair and shuts her eyes. Nina sets a huge pot of water on the stove and lights the burner with a match.

——————⊃◦⊂——————

After an excellent supper of chicken paprikash and cucumber salad with sour cream, Maxim retires to the kitchen to clean up after the sizeable mess his sister and grandmother made. He places a portion of their meal in a baking dish with a lid and puts it in the oven for his mother to heat when she gets home from work about three in the morning. Maxim's mama is quiet in the kitchen, but the aromas of her late supper often rouse him to consciousness. If he is not hungry, he rolls over on the futon mattress beneath his Steinway A and slides back to sleep. When he is hungry, he joins his mother for a snack of leftovers at the small kitchen table.

Maxim makes headway on the supper dishes and the bloody dismemberment of the chickens when he is startled by their loud door buzzer. Nina answers and Maxim strains to hear who it is.

"It's for you, Max. It's the photographer. Should I buzz her in?"

"No," Grandma says. "It's too late for visitors. You go downstairs, Maxim."

He wonders that she considers 8:30 in the evening late in a place like New York. He dries his hands and puts down the towel, checking that he has the check for Miss McGuirk in his wallet.

She stands in the elaborate marble lobby whose former elegance is now dull and a bit battered. Traces of illegible graffiti remain in layers one over the other. Phaedre is dressed in the same sleek red dress she wore to the photo shoot at Steinway Hall that morning. She does not look the least ruffled or wilted, whereas Maxim finds the steamy lobby oppressive and is beginning to soak his undershirt with sweat for the second time that day.

"It is past my grandmother's bedtime, I'm afraid," he tells her.

"Why don't we walk to the park? It's a beautiful breezy evening," Phaedre suggests.

He accepts the thick envelope from her and holds open the heavy beveled-glass lobby door. They walk up the steep incline of 181st Street to Fort Washington Avenue and turn north to Bennett Park. It is full of people: kids on bicycles and skateboards, old Jewish couples carrying on emphatic conversations, and two men holding hands at the dark end of a bench between street lamps. Maxim shows Phaedre to a spot on an unoccupied bench directly beneath a light. He waits for her to be seated.

"I'm very excited to see the photos, Miss McGuirk" he tells her, fumbling to get the envelope flap open. "I felt so strange standing in the room where Rachmaninov once stood. I'm glad I didn't have to play in Steinway Hall today. I was so nervous."

"You did fine," Phaedre assures him. "You looked very handsome."

Maxim's face grows warm. He hopes there is not enough light to show him blushing. Phaedre nudges closer and leans over him to peer at the glossy black-and-whites. He looks them over slowly, one by one, while Phaedre points out the salient features of each.

"Your glasses make you look just a little bit nerdy, but more handsome, in my opinion," she tells him.

Maxim thinks it's getting warm out again. The breeze has dropped.

"Please don't use that word," he remarks. "My sister is always calling me nerdy."

"I didn't know you had a sister. Here in New York?"

Maxim nods, looking over at Phaedre, close enough to kiss, if she'd invite him.

"Well, I think nerdy is sexy. I like this next one the best," she tells him, as though she'd memorized their order. "What's your favorite, Max?"

He is a little surprised by Phaedre's familiarity, but can think of no way to politely get her to refrain from using his nickname.

"I like the full-length photo," he tells her, "standing with my hand on the piano."

"But you look so serious in that one. You're almost scowling." Maxim laughs.

"Do you know what Stravinsky called Rachmaninov?"

"No. What?" she asks.

"A six-and-a-half foot scowl," he informs her, laughing again.

"Well, I think smiling is sexy, too," she tells him.

"It's getting late, Miss McGuirk. I don't want my family to think you kidnapped me."

Maxim puts the photos back in their envelope and stands up. He extends his hand to help her up from the park bench. She touches his sweaty hand. Hers is cool. Her red hair catches the light from the street lamp, like a glint from a fire.

"I think politeness is also sexy," she tells him. "But you needn't be so formal. You are very suave, Max. Very European. I like that."

Learning she lives in a basement apartment a block north of the park, Maxim walks Phaedre to her door. He takes her hand and bows. She smiles and her green eyes sparkle.

"Just a minute, Max," she says. "I have something I forgot to give you."

She enters the lobby and unlocks the door to her apartment. She returns a moment later with a printed flyer: "Circus McGuirkus - Performance Art."

"I hope you can make it. Please invite your sister. Complimentary, of course."

"Thank you, Miss McGuirk... I mean, Phaedre. I will do my best. When I am not playing, I am usually free on Fridays."

"I hope so. I think you will enjoy yourselves. Good night, Max."

Maxim turns and walks back down Fort Washington Avenue, holding the flyer in his damp hand. Phaedre watches him until he is out of sight around the corner on 181st Street.

Maxim's mother, home from work early, asks, "Where have you been, Maxim? We thought that photographer kidnapped you."

The women of his family sit side by side on the brocaded sofa. Maxim hands his mother the envelope containing his head shots. She opens it and flips quickly through the photos, then passes them one by one to her daughter. Nina hardly glances at them before passing the pictures to her grandmother.

"I had to look at each photo carefully before I paid her," Maxim explains. He touches the back pocket of his jeans where he keeps his wallet. "I forgot to pay her."

"Good thing," his mother says. "The pictures are dreadful. She'll have to do them over."

"At no charge," Nina adds.

"You should never trust a red-haired woman," his grandmother chimes in. "They are loose women, street-sweepers."

"Do you think she dyes her hair?" his mother asks no one in particular.

"I don't think so," Nina says. "That's probably the color the wig came in."

The three women cackle like the witches in Verdi's opera *Macbeth*.

Maxim stands holding the jumble of disordered photos. He stomps off to his piano room and draws the curtains. Slumping down on the bench, he feels as though he's been punched in the stomach. The three women continue their chatter and laughter even after he turns his lights out and crawls onto the futon mattress he unrolls beneath his Steinway A.

He struggles to fall asleep, wondering how his grandmother knew Phaedre's hair is red. Grandma likes to play the ignorant peasant, the superstitious *babushka*. But she is wily and clever and knows more about the world than he'd ever learned in school. Chickens on the subway! Maxim suspects it had less to do with obtaining the freshest poultry and more to do with some sort of divination.

Maxim had twice come home early and surprised his grandmother as she waved a fan of chicken feathers over three candles, wafting the smoke from sage incense and intoning what struck his ears as eerie chanting.

"Something smells bad in here," had been her explanation. "I'm waving it away."

At last his fading thoughts turn from Grandma's Old World practices to Phaedre's red hair. After reviewing each of her attributes, Maxim decides he likes everything about Phaedre, and that thought brings him to a most pleasant dream. The white noise of constant traffic on the Bridge washes over him, lapping like the waves on the Odessa beach when he was a boy.

Maxim decides to take Phaedre's suggestion and brings his sister along to the Friday performance at Circus McGuirkus. Nina seems to have a better idea of what is going on. To Maxim, New York City is the strangest part of a bewildering country. He has no idea what "performance art" is about. *Isn't all art a performance?* he wonders.

The performance space is a shabby old building on The Bowery, nearly the opposite end of the island from Washington Heights. Maxim and Nina are nearly late.

Circus McGuirkus shares the ground floor with another storefront, the King Herod Day School. Nina finds that funny but is unable to explain the joke to Maxim. They follow the crowd at the Circus to the stairwell. After descending several flights of stairs on the rickety staircase, they reach the performance space.

It is a small room with bare-brick walls and dimly lit by fancy crystal wall sconces. The uneven floor is painted concrete made to resemble polished marble. The seats are old theater chairs bolted to wooden planks. Maxim and Nina find their places.

Looking at the playbill, Maxim figures the production of *Homonym* must be about gay people. He is not delighted by the prospect, but he's sure Nina will find it trendy and delightful. She is wearing a green dress that matches her shoes and small handbag. Maxim is struck by the fact that his sister is grown up and very attractive.

The house lights dim. The red velvet curtains with gold tassels open. Onto the low stage walks a naked man painted entirely red and wearing a red ribbon tied around his very public privates, thereby confirming Maxim's suspicion. He braces himself.

The naked man carries a red violin and bow, but Maxim notices the violin has no strings. Then Phaedre walks onto the stage and stands next to the man. She is wearing a sleek red dress with a huge red bow tied at her waist. Phaedre touches the man's shoulder and turns to the audience.

"This is my boyfriend," she says, "my beau," and gives his red ribbon a playful tug.

Maxim is crestfallen. *Phaedre has a boyfriend? Or is it merely his stage role?* he wonders. The audience laughs. He turns to his sister for an explanation, but the naked man raises the red violin to his shoulder and takes up the bow as though he might begin playing.

"I'll explain when it's over," Nina tells her brother.

The man appears to bow the violin properly while his fingers race up and down the neck. He stops frequently in mid-stroke to bend at the waist, his fiddle at his side, to take numerous bows. Phaedre applauds him and the audience gets into the spirit. Then the man resumes "playing."

This goes on for too long a time, Maxim thinks, for the musical joke to be anything but tiresome. He perks up a bit when a small rowboat moves from behind the black backdrop. Maxim realizes it is only the front part of the boat, the bow. A sea captain in full regalia nudges it along until he is on the opposite side of the naked man from Phaedre.

An Indian, in his full-feathered regalia, approaches from behind the backdrop, raises his bow, and takes a rubber-tipped arrow from the beaded quiver on his back. He takes aim at the naked man and shoots him while he plays the silent violin. The man, struck in the chest, collapses to the floor and the lights go down.

When the lights come back up, the entire cast, with their bows and bows and beaus and bows, takes a bow. The audience laughs and applauds until Maxim thinks he is the only person in New York who doesn't understand performance art. He turns to Nina.

"You still don't get it, do you, Max?" she asks, studying his bewildered face.

"Of course, I do. It's about a homosexual ménage a trois. I just don't get Phaedre's part in it."

"Well, you can ask her. Here she comes."

Phaedre, minus the enormous red bow, rushes up to Maxim and Nina, taking both their hands.

"This must be Nina. She is as beautiful as you are handsome, Max. Thank you both for coming this evening. There's going to be little after-party at my apartment uptown. I'd love it if you could both come."

Maxim and Nina look at each other.

"All right," Nina says. "Please. What is your address?"

"Max knows where I live."

"Oh, he does, does he?"

"If you'll hang around a minute, I'll join you for the ride uptown," Phaedre tells them.

"What about your boyfriend?" Maxim asks.

"Oh, him," Phaedre says, chuckling. "Phil's just an actor. I hired him."

"Of course." Maxim says. "We'll wait for you upstairs."

Nina pokes her brother.

"You really are a nerd," she tells him. "You don't just look like one."

Maxim feels a bit ashamed about not having a clue what was going on, but Nina was the last person to whom he would admit that.

Maxim manages to snare a seat on the subway for Nina and Phaedre at West 4th Street for the long ride uptown on the A train. He stands in the aisle beside them. He thinks they are carrying on like schoolgirls, giggling and chattering like friends who've known each other all their lives. Once the train goes express after Harlem, he cannot make out a word of their conversation above the continuous roar of the train.

He sees himself in the darkened windows of the subway car. *Yes, a six-foot scowl*, he thinks. No wonder Nina makes fun of him. He takes himself too seriously. Maxim wonders what Phaedre truly thinks of him.

They emerge at 181st Street. Maxim walks between the two women as they climb the steep hill up Fort Washington Avenue to Phaedre's basement apartment. They carry on their conversation, speaking around and past Maxim as though he were a room divider.

Phaedre's apartment looks like the comfortable hangout of a person who wears many artistic hats. In addition to computer screens and an array of photographic equipment, there are shelves of handmade pottery, a guitar and banjo in the corner, and an electronic keyboard along the dining room wall. Maxim laughs to himself, thinking of his own "piano room." He hopes she does not ask him to play it. He detests musical "appliances."

"Max, would you mind playing something for us this evening?" Phaedre calls from the kitchen, nodding towards the keyboard.

"I'd be happy to," Maxim replies.

"But first a drink," Phaedre says. "Before the others get here. They're a lively bunch. I'm not sure how long the booze will hold out."

Phaedre carries a tray of ice and glasses, a bottle of expensive Russian vodka, and a scotch whisky called Old Curmudgeon. Maxim wishes his sister were at home. He feels wound up tight and would like to relax and enjoy the evening—and Phaedre's company. She invites them to sit on her lumpy sofa and pours Maxim a healthy dose of vodka, as though reading his wishes. She pours a thimbleful of scotch for herself. Nina has a "Pepski."

Maxim tosses a token ice cube into his glass and takes a good swallow of his vodka. He's pleased to note the bottle of *Fonarnoye Toplivo* (Lantern Fuel) has only just been opened. Phaedre asks him what he thought of the evening's performance at Circus McGuirkus.

"Unlike anything I've seen before," he replies, pleased he does not have to lie to her.

Nina asks the way to the bathroom. Maxim hopes she takes her time.

"And how do you like the vodka? It was the brand your

grandmother recommended."

"You know my grandmother?" Maxim asks, and nearly swallows wrong.

"Yes," Phaedre replies. "Your grandmother and I have known each other for a while. We met down in Union Square at the weekly farmers' market, in the stall of the guy who sells live chickens."

Maxim chokes on his vodka. Phaedre pours him a glass of water.

"We both like our poultry fresh," she remarks, "although I let the farmer kill and gut mine. I don't want to get attached to the chicken, you know, like a pet, on the long subway ride back home, though the fresh eggs would be nice."

The raucous door buzzer nearly startles Maxim out of his skin. Phaedre gets up from her chair to answer the door. Maxim decides to stand, too.

"Pour yourself another drink if you'd like, Max. I'll be right back. There's more Pepsi in the fridge for Nina."

There's a commotion of shuffling feet and laughter in the hallway as a half-dozen people spill into the apartment. Maxim pours himself a little more vodka over ice. He feels his first drink and decides to go slow. The buzzer buzzes again and suddenly the apartment is crowded. Maxim thinks a few faces look famil-iar, from the little theater down on The Bowery, but they seem to be wearing heavy makeup and fantastical costumes. Twice he mistook another man for a woman. He feels out of his element. Maxim wishes Nina would hurry up in the bathroom. He needs to use it himself and he does not want to be alone among these strange people.

The bathroom is unoccupied. Maxim wonders where his sister is.

When he returns to the living room, there is no place to sit. He recognizes no one from before, as though this were the second shift of Phaedre's quirky friends. His head is swimming as though he were on the verge of being falling-down drunk. There are so many people in the apartment he would have no place to fall. All the floor space is occupied. He catches Phaedre's eye.

"Have you seen my sister?" Maxim asks her, raising his voice to be heard above the conversational din.

"She left over two hours ago, and said she was going home."

"Two hours ago? We haven't been here that long."

Phaedre raises her chin and laughs.

"Maybe now might be a good time to play for our guests, Max, before they decide to go home. It's after midnight."

"After midnight? What's going on?"

"I suspect you're having a good time. Time flies when you're having fun, Max," she tells him. "Here. Your grandmother told me to give you these."

Phaedre hands Maxim the first and last pages of a musical score: *Piano Fantasy No. 12 in G, Maxim Andreyevich*.

"What is this?" he says. "A joke? The composition date is twenty years in the future. I've never composed a note in my life. Besides, all the middle pages are missing. "

Phaedre smiles.

"Your grandma just said to give it to you, that you'd figure it out. If it's too difficult, play something else, Max. What about that second piece you played at Steinway Hall?"

"OK. Give me a moment," he asks, poring over the two pages of the score, the beginning and the end. He likes the tune, impressed with his future musical abilities, beyond anything he imagines he'd ever accomplish.

Maxim weaves his way through the crowd towards the dining room where the small electronic piano sits against the wall. On the drinks table he sees that the ice in the bucket is completely melted. He is pleased to note that the bottle of vodka remains nearly full, but is puzzled about the strange, light-headed feeling that has overtaken him.

The *Fantasy in G* is not an easy piece and Maxim wonders whether he should attempt playing it after a single quick perusal of the first and last pages of the score. The theme is beautifully and deceptively simple. But he knows he is no good at improvisation. How is he to arrive at the recapitulation of the theme by the final page of the score? How will he bridge the wide gap?

Phaedre begins his introduction to the crowd of actors

and other oddballs filling her apartment. She has the talent for exaggeration of an impresario. Maxim doubts he'll be able to live up to his billing. Applause fills his ears, and he is sure he's blushing. But he cannot let Phaedre down. He pulls a dining chair up to the keyboard and places the two-page score on the music desk. *At least*, he thinks, *G. Schirmer, the music publisher,* his *publisher twenty years in the future, is still in business.*

The theme is in Maxim's head. He takes a deep breath and touches the keys. The theme is in his fingers. He closes his eyes and does not look at the score. His fingers fly across the keys. In all his years of practice and playing, he has never felt this strangely connected to the music he was producing, music he was making up on the spot.

On the wall above the electronic piano hangs an oil painting that reminds Maxim of the Odessa Gardens. It draws him in. He thinks he can smell the cypress trees. He glances down at the signature: Cyril Andreyevich. His father.

No, it cannot be, he thinks. *I am not myself tonight.*

Maxim wonders fleetingly whether Phaedre slipped something into his drink, even though he watched her pour it from a newly opened bottle. *But what about one of the other guests? Who? His sister?* Nina often plays pranks on him.

These thoughts intrude and find their way down to Maxim's long, slender fingers. They add strains of mystery and slightly sinister playfulness, a teasing he is in no hurry to satisfy. He lets his strange mood guide his hands. In his thoughts, he dedicates his performance to his father.

The music is not only about sound, he discovers. Music is a form of energy that engages all the senses. He realizes that his idea resembles the theory of some crackpot Soviet scientist like Velikovsky. Maxim feels he is melting into the eerie, shifting, pulsating room around him. He is only understanding music for the first time. It thrills him as never before.

Knowing he controls the music through his mind—his inner ear—and his fingers, he recalls the closing measures of his *Fantasy in G* and coaxes the theme along, untying the knots and pulling up the loose threads he has left. The final chords resound in the silent room.

When Maxim turns around on the bench to face the crowd assembled, he thinks he is looking at guppies in a fish bowl: all wide eyes and mouths hanging open.

Phaedre, standing in a corner, turns up the lights. He sees she has been crying. So have many of the others. That's why their eyes look glassy like fishes' eyes. He stands up and smiles, taking a slight bow. To his relief, applause breaks out. Phaedre comes forward and kisses his cheek. He knows he has woven her thread through his *Fantasy in G*, too.

She stares into his eyes, not removing her gaze for what seems to Maxim a long while. He is frozen where he stands, as though she has put a spell on him. He is embarrassed, and hopes the audience will think this one of Phaedre's performance pieces. When he next looks away from her, he sees the room is empty.

"What's going on, Phaedre? Where is everybody?"

"They left an hour ago. Are you all right, Max? Should I call your sister?"

"No. I feel so odd. Did you put something in my drink?"

"I'd never do that, Max. Maybe those leaves in the bottle didn't agree with you."

"What leaves?"

She takes him by the hand to the kitchen and shows him the nearly full bottle of vodka on the drain board of the old cast iron sink. There's a sprig of a plant inside that looks a little like rosemary or lavender.

"Kind of like the worm they put in the tequila bottles," Phaedre remarks.

"That brand of vodka does not come with a plant inside, nor any brand I know of."

"Take my word for it: the leaves were inside all along. You saw me struggle to get the bottle open. I think you were more interested in the vodka, Max. That's why you didn't notice the plant. And you were so nervous."

Maxim shrugs.

"Ask your grandmother, Max. She brought me the bottle of vodka. Would you like to spend the night? I'm worried about you."

"I would like to stay with you, Phaedre, but not tonight. I don't want them to worry."

As forward as any American, Maxim wraps his arms around Phaedre and plants a slow kiss on her lips. She does not resist, instead slipping her tongue into his mouth. This startles him, but he plays along, tussling with her tongue. His hands slide down her hips and thighs. He feels his resolve to leave melting.

"You're right, Max. Maybe next time. But just so you know, I really like you. And that piece you played tonight was the most beautiful, moving music I have ever heard. Really. And my friends loved it, too. You saw them."

Phaedre opens her front door and leads Maxim through the lobby and onto the street. He takes her hand and bows, then turns and walks back down Fort Washington Avenue. As before, she watches him until he turns the corner.

Maxim's feet do not seem to quite reach the pavement. He floats a few inches above, uncertain whether from the wonderful music he played that night or because of his growing affection for Phaedre. He decides it is on account of both, and floats homeward.

Tiptoeing down the hallway as soon as he leaves the elevator, Maxim reaches for his key ring. Just as he is about to put the key in the lock, the door swings open. Grandma pulls him inside and kisses both his cheeks.

"Dear boy," she tells him.

She is still wearing her frumpy black dress and her white American shopping sneakers. She is slightly stooped. Her gray hair is still in long braids beneath her babushka.

"I am sorry, Grandma. I didn't mean to make you worry."

"I was not worried, Maxim. I knew you were in good hands."

She coaxes him over to his Mama's white sofa and they sit down.

"I thought you did not like Phaedre," Max says.

"Just a performance, Max. I like her very much. I learned the fastest way to get two young people to fall in love is to forbid them to see each other. You will marry Phaedre, my boy."

"How do you know all this, Grandma? Do you practice magic?"

"Yes, practice is the right word. But I am getting better all the time."

"Did you put the plant in the vodka bottle? Please. Be honest, Grandma."

"I never lie, child, though I've learned the truth is a little squishy, a bit like bread dough. Yes, my friend Nikolai put the plant in the bottle without opening it."

Grandma gets up to prepare their tea. She serves it *a la Russe* in clear glasses and sweetens it with honey from the beekeeper down on Union Square. Maxim would not be surprised if she brought a live hive home on the subway next time. He waits for his tea to cool; Grandma takes a sip straight off, and smiles at him.

"I wanted you to see more clearly, Maxim, to relax and to take joy in playing. The special herb came from my friend Nikolai. Maybe you remember him from the Old Country."

"The skinny old fellow with long gray-and-white whiskers? He reminded me of a famous picture of Tolstoy."

"That's him. He helped me with bringing your music score back from the future, too."

"But why just the first and last pages, Grandma? I had to improvise the entire middle."

"I guess I misunderstood what Nikolai taught me. When I reached into the future and grabbed your music from the music store, I got only the cover and the pages just inside the cover, the first and last pages. I didn't want to bother Nikolai again to help me get your music. I want to save his help for getting your father out of prison. I thought you'd have to learn to improvise sooner or later. Why not sooner?"

"I'm not sure I believe in magic, Grandma. But that would be wonderful if Nikolai could get my Papa out of jail. I would love for my father to hear the music I can make."

Grandma clears her throat and refills their tea glasses, scooping honey into each.

"That's another thing, Maxim. I do not want to hurt your feelings. You are an excellent pianist, but you will never be a great one. Instead, you will leave your mark as the best American composer since Charles Ives."

"But I am Russian," he protests, sitting straighter.

"Yes, but your music will be American. Phaedre will be your promoter. Your music will bring much joy to a great many people, American and Russian. We will be proud of you. You will never become wealthy, but you will always have enough. You and Phaedre will live out your lives together, rich beyond measure."

"Thank you, Grandma. Thank you for telling me that. Did you read my music from the score? Did you like it?"

"I find it easier to learn magic from Nikolai, dear boy, than to learn to read music. Perhaps they are both magic and both music. Nikolai hummed your melody to me. It made me cry, Maxim. And there was also a very wonderful future review of your *Piano Fantasy in G* clipped to the first page, but I didn't want it to go to your head so I kept it."

Maxim laughs. "I hope I can remember what I played tonight. It made me feel like a musical magician weaving a spell over everyone."

Grandma smiles and stands up.

"You will remember it when the time comes, Maxim. But you will remember little else of tonight."

"Is there something in the tea?"

"Yes. And you'll remember that the piano your Grandma bought you with hoarded rubles is to be used only for music composition from now on, not for merely imitating the music of others. Your Mama will fight you on this, Maxim. You will have to work very hard to win her over."

Grandma dims the living room lamps and walks to her bedroom, the one she shares with Nina.

"And what about Phaedre? Will I remember how I feel about her in the morning?"

"Of course you will, Maxim. Love is its own magic, impervious to all other kinds. You will love her even more tomorrow."

"Good night, Grandma. Thank you. Are you sure I won't

remember any of this?"

"You will not remember, Maxim. The time is not yet right. Good night, child."

Maxim watches her shadow retreat and hears her bedroom door open and close softly. He goes to his piano room and pulls the drapes shut. He turns off the lamp and undresses down to his undershorts and T-shirt. He touches his Steinway A in a slow, loving caress, the lights of the Bridge reflected in its gloss. He wants to sit down and bang out what he still recalls of his future *Fantasy in G*, but he is too tired, and does not want his mother to hear complaints from the neighbors.

He unrolls the futon and scuttles beneath the piano. It is like a canopy bed of polished wood. Shutting his eyes, he hears music from inside him, something different, something not from his *Fantasy in G*. It is Phaedre's theme, his Opus 1. He intends to recall that snippet of music in the morning and jots notes on a blank sheet of score paper.

Maxim drifts to sleep thinking of how he and Phaedre will make love beneath his Steinway A when he plays the theme for her the next time Grandma goes looking for bargains down in Union Square on the A train.

JUST FRIENDS

Maxim's girlfriend, Phaedre McGuirk, wants to meet for drinks after work. He must travel down to The Bowery from 181st Street to her favorite tavern, The Ornery Burro. It is just around the corner from Circus McGuirkus, Phaedre's little performance company. He'd hoped to work on his newest composition in the afternoon, a jazzy opus dedicated to Phaedre as every piece had been for the past three months. The only other work had been inscribed to his father. At the last instant, he goes back for his notebook in case any ideas occur to him on the long ride to the opposite end of Manhattan on the A train.

The subway is hot and crowded. Maxim manages to secure a seat only one station away, but he finds it difficult to concentrate. He closes his eyes and is soon rocked to sleep by the rhythmic swaying of the train. When he awakens, he is two stops into Brooklyn. He will be late meeting Phaedre.

Max is out of breath by the time he arrives at The Ornery Burro. He's only fifteen minutes late, but Phaedre is already talking to some guy at the bar in tight jeans and a leather jacket. Having little confidence in himself, Max's heart sinks. *This is when she dumps me*, he thinks.

"There you are, Max. I'd like you to meet my cousin, Fitz—Fitzgerald McGuirk."

Maxim is struck by Fitz's handsomeness. His hair is black and wavy and his face is sun-tanned—nearly Maxim's opposite. He bares a strong resemblance to his red-haired cousin. They invite Max to sit between them. Phaedre orders an Old Curmudgeon whisky.

Fitz extends his hand to Max. His grip is strong, and Max does not have weak hands.

As though noting Max's scrutiny of them, Phaedre says, "Our fathers are brothers."

"Care for a drink, Max?" Fitz asks. He is the same age as Phaedre, twenty-eight, but, unlike his cousin, he retains a brogue.

"Um... *Fonarnoye Toplivo* vodka, if you please," Max says to the bartender.

"Max informs me it translates as *Lantern Fuel*," Phaedre says to her cousin.

They laugh. They raise their glasses to one another. Fitz lifts his bottle of Irish beer.

"Phaedre tells me you recently switched from playing classical to jazz."

"Yes, I did," Max says. "They're equally unprofitable."

Phaedre's cousin smiles. "Care to give us a sample?" he asks Max.

"Stop it, Fitz. Let him enjoy his drink."

"I don't mind," Max says, taking a swallow of his vodka on ice and approaching the Story and Clarke baby grand on a raised platform in the lounge.

Unlike most Russians, Max has a jazz musician's instincts, something innate that cannot be taught. He clearly enjoys performing for Phaedre and her cousin. It is just three months since he took up jazz seriously, but he feels at home improvising around any musical idea he hears.

A minute into Max's jazz piano solo, urged by Phaedre, Fitz joins him on the low stage. Max seems surprised. Fitz points to the conga drum in the corner. Max smiles and nods his head. Fitz plays the conga with the heel of his hand and fingertips, like tabla, taking his cues from Max. They go on for more than ten minutes, winding in and out among the strands of the theme Max has presented.

"You guys are hired," Lloyd, the night bartender, says. "When can you start?"

"We've never practiced together before," Fitz tells him.

"You could've fooled me," Lloyd replies.

Fitz orders Max another "Lantern Fuel" vodka, a whisky for Phaedre, and a beer for himself.

"On the house," Lloyd says.

"You guys were great," Phaedre tells them. "That was an amazing duet. Listen. I'm going to be gone over the Fourth of July weekend: a photo shoot in Sarasota. You guys can use my place to practice. I've got an electronic keyboard, bongos, and two *bodhrans*, Irish skin-drums."

"Thank you," Max tells his girlfriend. "That's great. After Fitz's playing, I'm convinced percussion is the right second voice."

"What do you say, Fitz?" Phaedre asks her cousin. "Max has been looking for someone to accompany his jazz piano solos."

"Your style of drumming would be exactly right, Fitz," Max tells him.

"OK, Max. You got a deal. I'll leave work early on Friday. We can meet at Phaedre's apartment around one o'clock, all right?"

"I'll be there," Max tells him.

Fitz kisses his cousin's cheek and shakes Max's hand.

"I'll see you, Cuz" he tells Phaedre. "I'm bushed; gonna head home. Maybe you can fill our calendar with gigs. Great meeting you, Max."

Max watches Fitz leave The Ornery Burro. He has a slight swagger. Maybe his snug Levi's make him walk that way.

"Your cousin is so cool," Max tells Phaedre.

"You know he's gay, right?"

"No, I didn't, but now I do," Max replies. "That certainly doesn't bother me. I think Fitz and I are on the same wavelength... musically, I mean. That's what's most important."

"I thought you'd like him. You two have sure got a unique sound. Care for another vodka?"

"No, I've had two. That's enough. How about you, Phaedre?"

"No, I'm good. Good night, Lloyd," she says, waving to the bartender.

Maxim helps her down from her stool. He holds the door for her and they walk to the subway at Chambers Street. When they hear the A train coming, they make a dash for the platform. They just squeak inside when the doors close on them. They have lost the thread of their conversation and do not even try to be heard above the din.

———————◦◦◦———————

Max and Fitz practice every chance they get, perfecting their sound. Phaedre offers her apartment for some of their sessions, often inviting a few of her friends to sit in on their musical gatherings. At other times, Max takes the 1 train up to The Bronx, spending the night at Fitz's place if their practice goes into overtime—which it usually does. A few times, on his way home from work, Fitz has picked Max up at Phaedre's apartment, giving him a ride on his Harley.

On the nights he stays at Fitz's place, Max sleeps on Fitz's sagging sofa. Phaedre does her best to curtail her jealousy, sorry whenever Max is not spending the night with her. She wonders whether there's something going on between her cousin and her boyfriend, but realizes it's a ridiculous notion. Max is as straight as any man she's ever dated and Fitz has been gay from the time they grew up in Ireland. She's a bit surprised by their burgeoning friendship but encourages it. They are the two most important men in her life and she wants them to get along.

Though Phaedre has gotten them several gigs in Manhattan, they all feel it's time to move on. Max and Fitz toy with the idea of her getting them engagements across the country, planning a tour from New York to California on Fitz's motorcycle. Phaedre doesn't want to discourage them. It is something Fitz has dreamed of since coming to America.

Fitz and Max decide to call themselves "Just Friends." Phaedre likes the name since it discourages the notion Max and Fitz are an item. By the middle of August, she has gotten them bookings as far out as western Ohio. The friends look forward to their road trip. Phaedre plans to join them as soon as she lands them an engagement longer than a few days.

The time for their departure arrives. Fitz plans on picking Max up from Phaedre's basement apartment on Ft. Washington

Avenue. Max frets about being away from Phaedre for so long, but he's also excited about seeing America and developing a musical following.

That afternoon, Max and Phaedre make love as though they will never see one another again.

"There's no point in getting dressed until Fitz gets here, Max. He said he's bringing all your gear."

"I've never owned a pair of Levi's or a leather jacket."

Phaedre's raucous door buzzer goes off, nearly scaring Max out of his skin.

Fitz is there to pick Max up. He has a package of duds for Max: new Levi's and longjohns, and an old pair of Fitz's biker boots, a faded jean jacket, and his old black leather jacket. Phaedre takes them to Max in the bedroom. The bundle is heavy.

"Fitz says to put everything on. The longjohns are to keep you warm on his Harley. It's supposed to be cool and rainy. I'll miss being with you, Max, but you can call me every evening if you like."

She places her arms around his neck and kisses him. Still naked, Max's little friend perks up.

"Not now," she admonishes, wagging her finger at his erection. "Haven't you two had enough? Save it until the next time we see each other, Max. Fitz wants to beat the traffic."

"It's going to be a long two months," Max tells Phaedre.

"It's going to fly by, you'll see. You're not going to have time to think about it, Max."

Phaedre rejoins her cousin in the living room. When Max emerges from the bedroom, the cousins look at one another and burst into laughter.

"Good God, you're a nerd, Max. You look like a plaster manikin dressed in cardboard," Phaedre remarks.

"Except for the boots and jacket, everything is stiff and starchy," he explains.

"Pray we get caught in the rain, Max, so they'll shrink on you. They'll get softer."

Fitz gives Phaedre a kiss on the cheek. Max enfolds her and kisses her until they are both breathless. They all leave Phaedre's apartment and walk to the curb where Fitz's Harley is parked. She contains her laughter at how awkwardly Max walks in his brand new shrink-to-fit Levi's.

"Don't worry, Cuz," Fitz tells her. "I'll take good care of Max."

"You'd better. I'm counting on you. And I want to hear that you two are so popular even I, your agent, won't be able to get tickets. I expect to hear a difference in your guys' playing by the time I catch up with you, too. Now, off with you. Don't forget to have a good time."

Fitz has a helmet for Max. He is barely able to straddle Fitz's bike in his stiff new jeans. They wave to Phaedre.

"Here we go, buddy," Fitz tells Max. "All you have to do is hold on tight and lean into the curves with me like we practiced."

Max scoots closer and takes hold of the belt of Fitz's black leather biker jacket. Phaedre hopes they continue to get along as well as they have been.

They pull away and head across the George Washington Bridge into New Jersey. Max is both elated by the feeling of flying and terrified by the thought of landing.

By the end of September, "Just Friends" approaches the eastern slopes of the Rockies.

Fitz and Max walk toward the Sea Breeze Motel office. They chuck each other on the shoulder, chuckling because the motor court is nearly smack-dab in the middle of land-locked New Mexico. Though they are several hundred miles from any body of salt water larger than a pickle barrel, there is plenty of breeze. The gale blowing into Española is dry and dusty. Their Levi's and leather jackets contain enough grit to qualify as sandpaper. They had a long ride that day on Fitz's Harley and they're saddle-sore and tired. Max dings the bell on the front desk.

Max, who's originally from Russia, thinks the rumpled old man who appears from behind the curtain resembles Tolstoy in his old age. To Fitzgerald, from Northern Ireland, the clerk looks like a skinny Father Christmas, though his long beard is more gray than white. The old fellow eyes them up and down with slit-eyed scrutiny.

"You bikers?" he inquires, closing the guest register and putting both hands on the counter.

"He is," Max tells the clerk, pointing to his friend Fitz. "I'm just his passenger."

The owner of the Sea Breeze Motel decides he must scrutinize them again in light of this new information. He strokes his long, pointed beard.

"Don't got no single beds. Just doubles, one to the room. You two OK with that?"

Before they can answer, the owner asks, "Are you fellows what they call *queers*?"

"I am," Fitz tells him. "But he's not," he adds, cocking his head towards Max.

The owner's puzzlement is written on his face in wrinkles and raised eyebrows.

"Ain't none of my beeswax anyway so long your money's good. I own this establishment. My name's Nicolás. That's thirty-nine bucks, plus New Mexico tax. Check-out's at 9:00 a.m. The wife's not as spry as she was and likes to get an early start. You OK with that?"

Fitz and Max both nod and reach into their Levi's to put up their half of the cash. Their money is dusty. Nicolás opens the guest ledger and asks to see identification. Fitz produces his New York State driver's license and Max shows him his passport.

"Fitzgerald McGuirk. You're a long way from home," the owner remarks. "What brings you to these parts?"

"Max and I are musicians. We call ourselves 'Just Friends.' We're going cross-country and landed a gig at The Ornery Burro in Red Willow."

"No practicing in your room," Nicolás admonishes them.

Max presents his passport. His hair is longer and a darker blond than in the photo.

"I can't read that Russian writing, son. Don't you got no

driver's license?"

"No, Mr. Nicolás. I don't drive. I'm just Fitz's passenger, remember?"

"Yes, you did tell me. In that case you can put down any name you like on the ledger. I got no way of knowing."

"We may be musicians and half of us are either queer or Russian," Fitz tells Nicolás, "but we are honest through and through."

"Nothing expressed or implied," Nicolás says to them. "There's the Sagebrush Diner across the road, closing in about twenty minutes, or there's the wife's goat stew. She's made too much again. I'm gettin' a little tired of it. You'd be helpin' me out."

Max and Fitz look at each other.

"We'll go for the stew," Fitz says.

"Ana will bring it to your room, Number 4, in about half-an-hour. Make sure you're dressed and decent."

Nicolás slides the key across to them, peering at them sideways. Then he vanishes behind the curtain to his quarters. Max and Fitz look for their room.

Fitz brings two of his remaining Harp lagers from his saddle bag. They are warm, but he does not care for cold beer anyhow. Max retrieves his bottle of vodka from the other bag.

Their room is typically Southwestern with a ceiling of *vigas* and *latillas*, tile floors, and thick adobe walls. The room is cool without air conditioning. The furniture, made of branches lashed together, is attractive but uncomfortable. Fitz removes his leather jacket in a cloud of dust. They sit on the edge of the bed and pour their drinks into paper cups on the night table.

"Sláinte," Fitz toasts, smiling at his friend.

"Za zdaróvye," Max returns, raising his Dixie cup of "Lantern Fuel" vodka.

"I wish we had more time before supper," Max complains. "I'd like to shower or at least shake my clothes out the open window."

Fitz combs his fingers through his wavy black hair and looks down at his dusty hand.

"Yeah," he tells Max. "But we can do that afterwards. The cost of supper is worth a little delay and discomfort, don't you think?"

"You're right. Let's raise a glass—Is that the expression?—to Nicolás and his missus."

"Yes, that's the right expression. To Nicolás and Ana," Fitz toasts.

Punctual to the approximate minute, there's a rap at the door of Number 4. Fitz gets up and opens it.

Ana enters with a tray containing two large ceramic bowls of goat stew and four thick slices of homemade bread. Like her husband, Ana is what Fitz has learned is called a mestizo, a mixture of Spanish and Indian. They are brown-skinned and, at this stage in their lives, gray-haired, worn in braids down their backs. Max takes the heavy, laden tray from the old woman, setting it on the single end table.

"Thank you, son. You boys are awful polite. Don't see that much these days. I don't know what my husband was worried about. Your appearance is a little ragged and dirty, but it's nothing a whole lot of water can't fix."

They laugh at her gentle ribbing.

"Thank you, Ana. We plan to shower before turning in," Fitz remarks.

"Enjoy your supper, boys. If you leave the tray outside your door, I'll pick it up when I go by. Enjoy your stay at the Sea Breeze."

Before Ana turns around, Fitz asks her a question, gravy dripping down his chin.

"How did this place come to be called the *Sea Breeze*?"

Max is getting ahead of him devouring his bowl of goat stew.

"Somewhere around a couple hundred million years ago or so, this area was on the shore of the Pacific Ocean, although back then it was called the Panthalassic Ocean. Nicolás unearths these obscure but interesting facts. I learn them just by being around him. So that's why we named it *Sea Breeze*: to honor the past."

"Thank you, Missus," Max tells her. "All sorts of useless information enters my head, too, just by hearing it."

"Oh, it's not useless, son. No knowledge is useless. You

never know when it might come in handy. And if you fellas are interested, I'm making flapjacks and corned beef hash for breakfast. I'll bring you some."

"Yes, please," Max and Fitz say simultaneously, wiping their mouths with their napkins.

"Of course, my husband says my flapjacks are rubbery and the hash is like dog food. He doesn't care for my cooking, but he's been putting it down his gullet for well over a half-century, and it hasn't harmed him any. Well, good night."

Ana slips through the door and closes it without a sound. Fitz and Max smile at each other and slurp down the rest of their stew, mopping up the gravy with the homemade bread.

"We haven't had to toss for who gets the bed in a while," Fitz says. "I think it's your turn to flip for it, Max."

"You can have the bed, Fitz. You did a lot of driving today," Max tells his buddy. "I can sleep on the floor on the chair cushions and the extra pillow."

"You sure?"

Max nods. He sits down in one of the wicker chairs, tossing his leather jacket over the back and tugging off his biker boots.

"Mind if I use the shower first, Fitz?" he asks.

"No, go ahead. Care for another drink?"

"Sure."

Fitz brings the Dixie cup and the bottle of vodka over to Max

"Want me to go look for some ice? I still got my boots on."

"Thanks, Fitz, but it's not necessary. Cheers," he says, raising his paper cup.

"Maybe we can call Phaedre in a little bit," Fitz suggests. "I'm sure you must miss her."

"I do, very much, but once 'Just Friends' has a confirmed booking, she'll be coming out here. I can't wait. I really like this part of America. I wouldn't mind living here."

"Me either," Fitz says, pulling the tab off his second Harp lager.

Max pours himself a little more vodka. Neither appears in a hurry to use the shower. They talk and laugh for an hour, trading stories and jokes, and musical ideas. They wind up falling asleep where they are: Fitz sprawled across the bed and Max slumped into the chair.

———————◦———————

Fitz awakens on top of the covers still in his clothes and boots. Max slouches in the wicker chair, also in all his clothes.

"Shit, Max. It's quarter till nine. We overslept," Fitz tells his friend, shaking him.

Max tugs his boots on and jumps up. There's a knock on the door. Fitz opens it.

It is Ana with a tray of flapjacks smothered in butter and syrup, the rest of each huge plate piled with a mountain of hash and a lava flow of fried egg yolk. On the side are two steaming mugs of black coffee.

"Bless you, Ana," Fitz tells her. "We overslept, more tired than we thought, I guess. I hate to eat in a hurry, but I get the idea your husband is particular about the check-out time. We can't afford a second day, I'm afraid."

"Oh, that," Ana says, clicking her tongue. "You take all the time you need."

She nods at the clock radio on the night table and then down at Max's and Fitz's wristwatches. It is now 8:15.

The friends smile at Ana. Though they are not sure how she performed that trick, they are grateful for the extra half-hour.

"May God grant you fellas safe travels. You are welcome anytime at the Sea Breeze."

"Thank you, Ana. God bless you, too," Max tells her as she goes out.

They sit on the bed with the tray between them and devour their breakfast as though they'd fasted the night before. Their coffee cups refill when they are not looking.

"This is a strange place," Fitz remarks. "And strange people. But they're friendly enough. Not like Anthony Perkins."

"Who?" Max asks his friend.

"From a Hitchcock movie. The actor played a motel owner who killed his guests."

"Glad I didn't see it. I like Nicolás and Ana."

"I do, too. I just happened to think of strange motel owners. Turn on the radio, Max. Let's hear what sort of weather we're in for today."

Max licks his fingers and swallows more coffee before switching on the clock radio. The forecast calls for thundershowers though the sky is crystal blue and cloudless. The male announcer reminds them it is monsoon season in New Mexico. Following the weather report, there is a radio quiz.

"Name the ocean that once lapped at the shores of New Mexico. The first caller to KROK with the correct answer will receive one-hundred dollars. The line is open."

Max puts the last piece of syrup-saturated pancake in his mouth and jumps to his feet. He dials the number the announcer gives his listeners. There is a busy signal. Max hangs up and dials again. A woman answers, repeating the quiz question.

"The Panthalassic Ocean," Max tells her, smiling from ear to ear.

"I won, Fitz. They want to know where to send the hundred dollars."

Fitz takes a ragged piece of paper out of his wallet.

"Have them send it to The Ornery Burrow in Red Willow," he tells Max, showing him the scrap of paper.

Max conveys the information and puts down the receiver, still grinning.

"Congratulations, buddy," Fitz tells Max, slapping his back. "I'll take our tray to the office. You stow our gear, OK? It's probably better if we head out right away if there's rain coming. We just night outrun it."

The friends meet at Fitz's Harley. They remark that the Sea Breeze had no other guests. They put on their dusty helmets. Max gets on behind Fitz, gripping the belt of his jacket, and they pull out onto the gravel road.

———————◦◦———————

Though it is barely a two-hour drive to Red Willow, they take several wrong turns and get lost. They remain almost as far from their destination as when they started out. Fitz pulls over beneath a stand of cottonwoods where there is shade to consult their maps. Max climbs off to walk around and stretch his legs.

"Uh-oh," he tells Fitz. "Look," he adds, pointing to the horizon.

A herd of thunderclouds seems to be stampeding towards them, accompanied by rumbling and frequent flashes of lightning. Fitz folds up the maps and stashes them in his saddle bag.

"Maybe we'd better hunker down here, Max."

"*Hunker?*" he asks.

"Crouch down. Lie low," Fitz explains.

"Not under these tall trees. It's dangerous."

"All right, buddy. So do we put on our raingear or take a shower?"

"We wanted to get clean last night, but never took our showers. The weather's warm enough, right?"

"Yeah, but we're at nearly eight thousand feet. The rain will be as cold as meltwater."

"That's all right," Max tells his friend. "I just want to get clean."

He climbs on behind Fitz. The Harley creates clouds of dust even as the rain clouds bear down on them. Before they have gone two miles, the sky opens up. The rain comes at them from all directions as though they were in a car wash. They get completely soaked. Hailstones clatter against their helmets.

Unable to see clearly, Fitz slows to a crawl and then pulls over as the torrent continues. There is no shelter anywhere in sight. They get off the motorcycle. Fitz takes off his helmet. The cold rain streams down his face in rivulets. Max removes his helmet so he can hear what his friend is saying.

"Might as well get our hair washed, too. Got any shampoo?" Fitz asks, laughing.

Max reaches into the pocket of his soaking wet Levi's and produces two small bars of motel soap. He offers one to Fitz. It is soft around the edges, but the wrapper has kept it from dissolving completely. They soap up their hair and then face into the wind and rain to rinse off, chuckling as they do so.

The thunderstorm trails away. The slanting rain no longer

reaches the ground.

"Glad we got rinsed off in time," Max says.

"From the look of it, there will be more opportunities," Fitz tells him.

The sun comes out overhead and they get back on the Harley. They go for a few miles, drying their hair, and then strap their helmets back on. Before long, they're dry everywhere except their backsides. Then the next wave of weather hits them and they get drenched again.

They dry out one more time in the wind and sun before a misty cloud descends on them. While it's not enough to soak them, Fitz finds it hard to see. He pulls in at the first neon sign he encounters, unsure what it is advertising. He and Max take off their helmets.

The sign reads, "Sea Breeze Motel."

"Can't be," Fitz remarks. "Are they a chain?"

"Or have we gone in a circle again?" Max suggests.

"Only one way to find out," Fitz says, shrugging.

They get off the motorcycle. It is clear to them that while the old adobe motel looks the same as the place they stayed the night before, its surroundings are quite different. There are more trees, cottonwood and aspen, and less scrub and sagebrush. They walk to the office, their boots still squishing a little.

The map on the counter, with *You are here* circled in red, shows them they are in Red Willow. Last night, it said they were in Española, but every other detail of the slightly shabby motel office remains the same. This time Fitz dings the bell.

Ana answers, flinging her long braids over her shoulders.

"Hello," she says, her face lighting up. "It's nice to see you fellas again. Didn't expect you so soon."

"Are we still in Española?" Fitz asks, though he knows they are not.

"No, this is Red Willow. Isn't that where you boys said you were headed?"

She turns the guest register towards them. Max and Fitz reach into the pockets of their slightly damp Levi's and come up empty-handed.

"I understand," Ana tells them. "You can pay me later."

"As soon as we go see the owner of The Ornery Burro for our audition, we'll get a week's advance," Fitz says, adding, "if we get the gig, that is."

"You will pass your audition," Ana says. "I'm sure of it. Don't worry."

"Thank you, Ana," Fitz tells her. "I hope you're right."

She smiles at them. Nicolás appears from behind the floral curtain to their living quarters. Fitz and Max sign the register. The old man looks down his half-spectacles at them.

"Well, you fellas look a sight better today. Been to the laundrymat?"

"Yes," Max tells him. "Nature's own laundry. It's called a thunderstorm."

"They got caught in the downpour, Nicolás. Don't make fun. If you fellas give me your wet duds later, I'll dry 'em for you."

"You have a clothes dryer?" Max asks.

"Just a clothesline, but it's always sunny above my clothesline. Your stuff'll be dry in no time at all."

"Bless you," Fitz tells her.

Nicolás checks their signatures against their entries of the night before and hands them the key to Number 4.

"The others are all taken again, I'm afraid," Nicolás informs them.

"That's quite all right," Fitz says. "It was a pleasant room and we sure slept like stones."

Fitz parks the Harley in the usual spot and Max goes to Number 4. Fitz finds his last Harp lager and his friend's vodka in the saddle bags and takes it to their room. He finds Max already stripped out of his clothes, a towel wrapped around his waist. Fitz gets undressed as well and also dons a towel, but then he puts his biker boots back on. They hang their wet leather jackets over the uncomfortable wicker chairs.

Fitz takes their bundle of damp clothes to the yard behind the Sea Breeze office. Ana watches him step across the yard in his tall black boots and white towel, shirtless.

"Men are such boys," she mutters to herself.

Fitz tosses the clothes over the wash-line and helps Ana pin them. Each time he reaches for a clothespin, his towel slips and he grabs it before it falls to the ground. The clothes hang at crazy angles and the wooden clothes-pins are all askew. When Fitz returns to Number 4, Ana re-pins every item Fitz hung on the line.

Back in their room, Fitz tells Max, "It really is sunny above Ana's clothesline. Won't take long at all to dry our stuff."

"And then what are we going to do?" Max asks, irritation in his voice. "We're out of money, Fitz. What are we going to do for supper?"

"I haven't thought ahead that far, buddy. One problem at a time, OK?"

"OK."

They pour themselves a drink in paper cups, careful not to hold them too firmly. There's a knock at the door. The friends look at each other. Fitz gets up to see who it is, holding his towel. Ana stands there with a wicker laundry basket full of their clothes, all neatly folded.

"Here are your things," she announces. "You boys are old-fashioned, wearing longjohns. Even my Nicolás wears shorts in summer."

"Keeps us warm on the Harley," Fitz tells her, putting their clothes on the bed.

"Of course," Ana replies. "I'm afraid my husband forgot to tell you about a phone call that came for you. From Phaedre."

"My cousin," Fitz says.

"My girlfriend," Max says.

Together they add, "How'd she know we were here?"

Ana shrugs and picks up the empty laundry basket.

"May we use your telephone?" Max asks.

"We don't have one," she tells them.

"Then how did...?" Max and Fitz say at the same time, stopping themselves short. Dumbfounded, they look at one another with befuddled expressions.

"They have a pay phone across the way at the Sagebrush Diner," Ana tells them. "But they're closing soon."

"Are they a chain?" Fitz asks.

"Never saw but that one," Ana replies. "Always on the other side of the road."

"Thank you, Ana. And thank you for drying our clothes," Max tells her.

"Wasn't me. It was the sun and the breeze, the Sea Breeze."

Ana smiles. She leaves their room, closing the door behind her.

In a hurry to use the pay phone before the Sagebrush Diner closes, Max and Fitz scramble into their clothes, skipping their longjohns and leather jackets.

"I think those are my Levi's," Max tells his buddy.

"What's it matter? It's not like one of us is short and the other's tall. We wear the same size for Pete's sake."

"Right," Max says. "What're we going to make the call with?" he asks, fumbling in the empty pockets of someone's jeans.

"I keep a few bucks at the bottom of my saddle bag. I'm never completely broke unless I forget to put back what I took out."

After retrieving his last ten-dollar bill, Fitz and Max head across the road. The fog is so thick they cannot see whether or not there's any traffic, but they don't hear anything coming.

Fitz wastes no time asking the cashier for change. She misunderstands, thinking he wants singles. Her name is embroidered on her white blouse.

"We need quarters for the pay phone, Fanny." Fitz says, as though he knows her.

"I don't think I got that many," she tells him, "but I'll give you all I can spare. If you talk fast maybe you won't use 'em all up."

"Thanks, Fanny. I appreciate the advice," Fitz remarks, his deep blue eyes smiling at her.

He hands the quarters to Max. Fitz dials Phaedre's number and hands the receiver to his friend. Phaedre answers on the second ring.

"I miss you so much, Phaedre," Max tells her. "When are you coming out here?"

Max jingles the quarters in his hand as he talks. He holds

the phone away from his ear so Fitz can listen in.

"I want to make sure you guys are booked for a couple longer gigs before I head out there. It's a long train trip from New York. I was getting worried about you guys. I didn't hear from you last night. Where are you, Max?"

"We fell asleep. We just pulled into Red Willow about an hour ago."

"What took you so long getting there?"

"Weather, mostly, and a couple of wrong turns."

"Are you having a good time, Max?"

"The time of my life. America is so beautiful in so many different ways. I like your cousin a lot, too," he says, grinning at Fitz. "There's only one thing missing."

"What's that?"

"You, Phaedre."

"You're so sweet, Max. How's Fitz? How's he behaving? Is he with you?"

"He's standing a foot away."

"To continue your call, please deposit seventy-five cents for the next three minutes," the nasally operator's voice intones.

Max hands the receiver over to Fitz who has been nervously shifting from one foot to the other. Max feeds the operator three more quarters.

"When are you going to see the owner of The Ornery Burro, Fitz?" Phaedre asks her cousin.

"We'll go see him tomorrow morning," Fitz tells Phaedre. "What's his name again?"

"His name's Plugg Uglie," Phaedre says.

"Before I forget, Cuz. How'd you know where we were staying?" Fitz asks her. "We didn't know it ourselves until we got here."

"I got the number from Max's grandmother. You didn't give it to her?"

Both men shake their heads.

"No," Fitz says to his cousin. "We didn't tell Max's grandma. We had no idea where we'd be stopping for the night."

"Please deposit seventy-five cents for the next three minutes."

Fitz looks to Max. He deposits their last three quarters.

"Put Max back on before you run out of time," Phaedre says to her cousin.

Fitz hands the receiver back to his buddy.

"It sounds as though you've had a long, strange trip, Max."

"*What a long, strange trip it's been* is a line from The Grateful Dead," he tells Phaedre.

"You've heard of The Grateful Dead in Russia?"

"Sure. There were Deadheads in Russia. Russia's hardly on the back side of the moon."

They hear the change settle into the belly of the telephone and the line goes silent. One by one the restaurant lights are turned off. Fitz and Max wave to Fanny and head back across the road to the Sea Breeze Motel. They can see their breath. Fitz puts his hands in his jeans pockets.

"I'm thinking of another song," Max says, pointing to the mist-shrouded pink and turquoise neon sign. "It was made popular by Dean Martin. Yes, we also heard of him in Russia."

He clears his throat and sings:

> "When you're down by the sea
> and an eel bites your knee,
> that's a moray."

Fitz nearly chokes with laughter and pauses to catch his breath. He pokes Max's shoulder.

"If you can make puns like that, buddy, you know way more English than you let on. That was pretty damn good. The only thing missing now is a nice, hearty meal."

"I've got some pretzels in my saddle bag," Max tells him.

They laugh.

"I don't remember leaving a light on in our room, Max. Did you turn one on?"

"I don't think so."

A wave of scrumptious aromas greets them as soon as they open the door of Number 4. There is tray of steaming food on the low end table. Max finds a note.

Dear Fitzgerald and Maxim.

We're all out of goat stew tonight, but our nephew bagged a couple of rabbits. My Nicolás has a soft heart and cannot bear the thought of eating them. I hope you like rabbit stew. I have saved two of their feet for your continued good luck.

Your friend,
Ana

"That is so sweet," Fitz remarks. "Just when I thought our luck had run out."

The friends sit down on the bed, placing the tray of food on the end table between them. They chow down like starving beggars.

"It looks like there are more mushrooms in her stew than rabbits," Max says. "I used to hunt mushrooms with my grandma back in Russia. She knows everything there is to know about them. That's who Ana reminds me of."

"She couldn't possibly because she reminds me of my grandma back in Ireland," Fitz tells him.

"Then we'll just have to share her," Max says.

Fitz smiles, mopping up some of the gravy with his bread and popping it into his mouth.

When they have finished their supper of rabbit stew, Max takes the tray to the motel office. There is no one around so he leaves it on the counter. By the time he gets back to old Number 4, Fitz has taken his boots and jean jacket off. He's sprawled out on the bed, his legs crossed, snoring as though he's sawing logs.

Trying not to disturb his friend, Max sits down in the wicker chair and tugs off his biker boots. One of them slips out of his hand and drops to the floor. The noise awakens Fitz.

"I'm sorry, buddy," Max tells him. "Are you turning in already?"

The clock radio on the bed table says it is only 9:15. Max

hangs his jean jacket over the back of the chair on top of his leather jacket.

"I am so sleepy," Fitz tells his friend. "I feel so strange. Not really high. It's more like the world is high and I'm only just now noticing it. I wonder if it was the mushrooms."

"I think maybe those red ones with the white spots were the kind my grandmother told me never to touch. Do you think Ana poisoned us?"

"Do you really believe that, Max?"

"No, but I feel very peculiar, too. Queer."

"No, you can't, Max. I'm the one who's queer."

They laugh. Fitz sits up at the edge of the bed and tugs off his socks. He ruffles through the neatly folded pile of their clothes.

"I think I'm going to call it a day," he says. "Do you know which are my longjohns?"

Both pairs look as though they've been tie-dyed from the indigo in their Levi's when they got drenched.

"I gave up trying to figure out whose clothes were whose back in Pennsylvania."

Fitz stands up to unbutton his Levi's when the telephone on the bed table rings. It is not plugged into the phone jack and does not even have a cord. The friends look at one another. Fitz reaches for the receiver.

"Hello?" he says. "It's Phaedre," he mouths to Max, who comes over and sits beside him.

"I got a call from the owner of The Ornery Burro tonight after I spoke with you and Max," Phaedre says. "He told me you guys passed the audition and can start on Friday, guaranteed minimum of three weeks. That's wonderful news. But I thought Max told me your audition isn't until tomorrow."

"That's right, Cuz, not till tomorrow. It must be the time difference. It's still Tuesday out here in New Mexico."

"I'm not sure what's going on. You've passed before you even had your audition? Put Max on, Fitz."

He hands the phone over to Max.

"Hello, my love. I still miss you so terribly. How are you?" he asks Phaedre.

"As well as can be expected without you next to me. But, now that you and Fitz will be signing a contract, I'll be coming out on the train early next week."

"Can't you fly, Phaedre?"

"No, I don't have enough for the plane. It's only a four-day trip, Max. If there's a train leaving Penn Station on Saturday, I might get there by late next Tuesday or early Wednesday. Be patient. I'll call you guys tomorrow. Good luck with your audition."

"We already got the booking, remember, Phaedre?" Max reminds her, laughing at their confusing situation.

"Oh, that's right. I'm the one who told you. Everything is so strange with you so far away, Max. Be good to each other until I get there."

"We will," they say, chucking each other on the shoulder.

Max hangs up the phone.

"Well, that's good news," Fitz remarks.

He strips out of his jeans and pulls on his longjohns. Following their custom, Fitz takes the wicker chair this time, propping his feet up on the end table. He covers himself with their jean jackets.

Max puts on his longjohns and climbs beneath the covers. He turns off the lamp on the bed table, which, like the phone, is not plugged into the outlet.

"Sleep well, my friend," Max tells Fitz.

"You know what I think, Max? I believe we are already asleep. None of this is really happening."

"You may be right. But am I in your dream or are you in mine?" Max asks.

"Yes," Fitz replies.

The song of crickets drifting through the open window lulls them to sleep. Max and Fitz are snoring in no time. Max dreams himself into Phaedre's arms; Fitz imagines a handsome man with hair so black it is almost blue.

———————————◦◦◦———————————

Phaedre arrives the next Wednesday on the Santa Fe Chief and what seems to her an even longer ride from the capital city aboard the shuttle bus. She does not find Max and Fitz in their room at the Sea Breeze Motel. She asks the desk clerk if she knows where they might be.

"They have been practicing every afternoon before The Ornery Burro opens," Ana informs her. "I didn't picture you quite so petite. You must be Phaedre."

"Yes, I am. And you must be Ana. The boys told me how kind you have been to them. Thank you. You look exactly like our grandmother. Fitz is right."

"I take that as a most generous compliment," Ana says, giving her gray braids a jiggle. "You are lucky to have two well-mannered and handsome men in your life. I had to settle for just one."

Ana and Phaedre laugh.

"Yes, I am very lucky indeed. They are smart and gentle and generous, too. I think it's to their credit that they're also best friends despite their many differences."

Ana hands Phaedre the key to "the fellas' room."

"You and Maxim will become husband and wife very soon," the old woman tells her.

"I think Max has to propose to me first."

"Oh, that he will, my dear. Before the day is done. Mark my word."

"In that, Ana, you are more like Max's grandma. Do you do magic?"

"No, child. It's more like magic does me. My husband, Nicolás, and I will be driving to The Ornery Burro tonight to hear Fitz and Max perform. You can ride with us."

"Thank you, Ana."

"In the meantime, you go freshen up and lie down awhile. Nicolás will bring the old pickup around in about an hour or so."

In the room, Phaedre takes two navy blue blazers from her suitcase and hangs them up on the hooks behind the door to Number 4. She smooths out their wrinkles with a damp washcloth. Then she lies down on the bed and closes her eyes. She dreams of Max proposing to her, but awakens before she's had a chance to accept.

Phaedre, a slender redhead, sits between Ana and Nicolás, holding the jackets for Max and Fitz in her lap. At The Ornery Burro, she hands the blazers to Nicolás and rushes up to Max. Phaedre wraps her arms around Max's neck and her legs around his hips. They twirl around until they are dizzy. The only thing to interrupt their frantic kissing is their laughter.

Fitz is at the bar chowing down on a burger. He waits until the lovebirds have had their time and gives his cousin a long hug and a short kiss. He orders a round of drinks: Harp lager, Lantern Fuel vodka, and Old Curmudgeon whisky for his cousin Phaedre. They smile and toast one another.

Nicolás brings the dark blue blazers to them.

"What's this?" Fitz asks Phaedre.

"Thank you, Nicolás. It's a change of image, Cuz. Max is too suave for a biker jacket. It wouldn't hurt you to dress up a couple notches, either."

She helps her cousin and her boyfriend into their blue blazers. Unnoticed by the others, Nicolás slips a tiny box into the pocket of Fitz's blazer and joins his wife in the lounge. He and Ana find two of their friends and engage in inaudible but animated conversation.

"I know you're too rough and tumble for dressy slacks, Fitz. That's not who you are. So you guys keep your biker boots and Levi's, but you dress it up a bit with the new jackets."

"Sounds worth a try, Cuz. What do you say, Max?"

"The leather jackets are a bit warm under lights, don't you think?"

"Yeah, you're right. OK, Phaedre. You got a deal."

"Good. I already told Plugg, the owner, that you'd agreed. I meant to tell you when we spoke for the second time the other night."

Max and Fitz look at each other, not sure what to make of the revelation that their shared hallucination was, in fact, the real deal. They *had* talked to Phaedre on the disconnected phone and she *had* told them what hadn't happened yet.

It is time for Fitz's and Max's performance. Tonight, Max takes the mic for their introduction. The lounge grows quiet; the lights go down.

"My pal Fitz here comes from Ireland. I am Max and I'm from Russia. He is gay and I am straight... or is it the other way around? It doesn't matter. We're a two-man quartet and call our-selves 'Just Friends.' We are best friends, in fact, and we're here to make the best music we can for you. May God bless you all with friendship, the real kind, that takes you exactly as you come."

There is hearty applause. Max sits at the well-tuned up-right and Fitz sets himself in the middle of an array of drums and gongs that are all played by hand. They jam together as they have not done before. On the downbeat, Max slams out a couple riffs that Fitz imitates. They answer each other back and forth, at times smiling at each other as though sportively trying to trip each other up. Their first number lasts a half-hour at a gentle full-tilt. They leave their audience breathless.

When it is time for their break, they walk over to Phaedre's table where she has been joined by Plugg. He wears expensive clothes that are all mismatched, making him look clownish.

Max and Fitz each kiss Phaedre and shake Plugg's hand.

"You guys were beyond terrific tonight," Plugg tells them.

"Thanks," the two friends say at the same time.

"Is it them new jackets or what?" Plugg asks. "Sort of grub-by chic, I'd call it. Here. This came for you, Max, from the radio station in Santa Fe. You guys gonna play in their studio?"

"No, it's a check," Max tells him, tearing open the envelope. "I won their quiz last week."

He hands the $100 check over to Phaedre, agent and man-ager for "Just Friends." He leans into her shoulder and gives her a kiss that only the presence of others causes him to restrain.

"We have to go play our next set," Max tells Phaedre.

He bows and kisses her hand. Apart from his dusty boots and Levi's, she thinks he looks almost elegant in his new blazer.

Back upon the low stage, Max asks Fitz, as he has not done before, to set the theme of their next number with his percussion.

"The piano is also a percussion instrument," Fitz reminds him.

Max's and Fitz's second set leaves the entire place spell-bound. It is music no one has heard before that is nevertheless familiar and friendly. Max's playing is urban and sophisticated, Fitz's rougher and less predictable. Their audience sit in stunned amazement at their unique sound and accomplished playing. They leave the crowd unable to express their delight in any way other than getting to their feet and applauding madly.

The grateful duo take their bows. Then Max asks for silence.

"A dear friend has come all the way from New York to hear us play tonight. Please come up, Phaedre."

Max kisses her on the cheek and continues.

"Phaedre is my buddy Fitz's cousin and, after tonight, I hope she will be my fiancé. What do you say, Phaedre? Will you marry me?" he asks, getting down on one knee.

She puts both hands over her mouth as though to contain her surprise. The Ornery Burro erupts with applause and laughter. Fitz hands Max the small velvet box Nicolás slipped into the pocket of his blazer. Max waits to open it.

"Yes, Max. I will marry you. Most certainly yes," Phaedre tells him.

Max rises and places the ring of nearly microscopic diamonds on her finger. The setting is an intricate Celtic knot. The crowd again shout and clap their approval. Max hugs and kisses Phaedre. Fitz hugs them both.

"One more thing," Max announces. "I think I'll ask my best friend to be my best man."

The patrons of The Ornery Burro holler their favorable reception of the idea. Then Max and Phaedre go among the crowd, shaking hands and accepting good wishes. Phaedre looks for the old couple, Nicolás and Ana, but she does not find them. *It is eleven o'clock: probably past their bedtime*, she thinks. She remembers the old woman's prediction about Max's proposal, and smiles.

Fitz sits down at the bar. While he is happy for Max and Phaedre, he feels a bit on the outside. A couple of men at The Ornery Burro near his own age caught his eye, but he's no idea whether they turn clockwise or anticlockwise. One of the men he has been admiring approaches. He is a lanky and handsome *mestizo* with a bronzed complexion and longish black hair.

"Excuse me," the man says. "An old couple I know who were here earlier asked me to give you this note. I've known Ana and Nicolás since I was a child."

"Thank you," Fitz says. "I know them, too. I'm staying at their Sea Breeze Motel."

The man hands Fitz the folded piece of paper. Fitz notices a welcoming smile in his deep brown eyes.

"Your playing was fantastic," the man tells him. "I belong to a drumming circle—on the Pueblo."

Fitz opens the note.

Dear Fitzgerald McGuirk,

    We hope you don't feel left out. This one's for you. We noticed that the bearer of this note had been admiring you this evening. Perhaps you two have something in common. We hope so. And we hope you don't mind our matchmaking.

          Love,
          Ana & Nicolás

Fitz is speechless.

"Good news?" the man asks.

"Yes," Fitz tells him. "Can I buy you a drink?"

"Sure. I'll have whatever you're drinking. My name's Antonio."

"I'm Fitz, as you know—short for Fitzgerald."

They shake hands. Fitz orders two dark beers from the local brewery. He and Antonio lean their elbows on the bar and begin getting acquainted. Phaedre is about to invite Fitz to join her and Max at their table, but turns on her high heels, deciding to leave well enough alone.

"I've actually seen you perform here a couple of times," Antonio tells Fitz.

"I thought you were a little bit familiar. I probably stared at you."

"That's OK. I never mind the attention of a handsome man, especially if he's wearing boots and Levi's."

"*La ropa hace al hombre,*" Fitz tells Antonio.

"Clothes make the man," he replies.

"Well, certain clothes—and certain men," Fitz remarks, turning his smile on high.

They clink their glasses of beer.

"Can you tell me a good place to stay?" Fitz asks Antonio. "Now that my cousin and my friend are engaged, it'd be a little awkward staying in their room, you know?"

"You're welcome to crash at my place, Fitz. Really. I've got a pretty comfy sofa in the living room."

"Sure it's not too forward on a 'first date,' know what I mean?" Fitz asks.

"Yeah, I do. I like a man with manners. But it's OK. Stay until you work something else out."

"Thanks," Fitz tells him. "I've already got another favor to ask."

"Shoot," he says, taking a swallow of his beer.

"Could you drop my cousin back at the Sea Breeze? I'll take Max on my motorcycle."

"Gladly. She's quite a beauty. My pickup is kind of grubby, though."

"She can sit on my leather jacket. It's over there, on the hook."

"Great," Antonio says, finishing the last of his ale and retrieving Fitz's jacket.

Fitz finishes his beer, too. He and Antonio walk over to the engaged couple to tell them the plan they have worked out.

The two couples separate in the gravel lot of the Sea Breeze Motel: Max and Phaedre to Number 4, and Fitz and Antonio to his old turquoise pickup. Fitz takes the note from the pocket of his blazer and scribbles on the back on the hood of the truck. He folds the note and slips it into the dropbox beside the motel office door.

Dearest Ana and Nicolás,

Thank you both for all you have done for me and Maxim and Phaedre—and, I hope, Antonio, too. I believe you have made 4 people very happy.

God bless you both.

Love,
Fitz

Fitz takes off his blazer and folds it inside out. Then he puts on his old leather jacket and climbs into the pickup, putting his new jacket in his lap. He and Antonio see the light go out in Number 4. They turn to each other and smile, possibly having exactly the same thought.

CLOTHES MAKE THE MAN

My clothes, like me, are a little tattered and frayed at the edges. My Levi's are worn shiny on the seat and thighs. One knee is nearly out. My leather jacket is abraded, the lining long ago ripped and pulled out. My jean jacket is now the lining. I don't wash my denims unless it's inadvertent: getting caught in the rain or pushed into a pond or fountain. The soles of my biker boots are as thin as my socks. All that aside, these are my favorite clothes. I've been into Levi's and leather since I was a teenager back in Northern Ireland ten years ago. I guess it's my fetish.

Though I don't look especially shabby—certainly not by American standards—inside my clothes I feel ragged: scraped and scarred by fortune's dings and arrows. Despite coming to New York five years ago, I still have not met the man of my dreams. I've begun to think my attire is to blame, that my clothes are sending the wrong signal. It seems that, more than anyone else, young women with tattoos and piercings and wild, dyed hair are drawn to me, those my grandmother would have called "trashy trollops." I think they are attracted to my gear, not the man inside. That is why I am about to embark on an experiment to change my appearance, something I do not take lightly. My clothes are who I am.

I suppose I am desperate since even my queer mates have been unable to find me my ideal man—or even a first date that led to a second. A couple weeks back, I consulted a white-haired palm reader. Her brightly-colored, billowing robes distracted me, but I wrote down as many of her utterances as I could recall upon returning to my fifth-floor apartment in The Bronx. She recommended a vintage clothing shop in Manhattan on Thirteenth Street.

I decide at the last minute to give the shop a try after work while I still have money in my pocket. I park my Harley at the curb.

They call themselves "The Vicarious Vicar." Their painted wooden sign is sun-bleached and the windows a bit grimy, but every item inside is carefully arranged upon racks by size and color. The wooden floorboards creak beneath my boots.

"Good evening, young fellow," the old man behind the counter says to me.

I hadn't noticed him. He closes a book he'd been reading and rests his hands on the polished wood counter All the items arranged on it seem to hark to the 19th Century, from the carbon-copy receipt book to the brass mechanical calculator and tortoise-shell fountain pen. His gray wool suit appears to be from the same era, as does he himself, though he'd have to be much older than he looks: well over a hundred. I'd have sooner wandered up and down the narrow aisles and not have anyone breathing down my neck.

"Please feel free to browse to your contentment. All questions are free to ask," he adds, smiling.

Yeah, but how expensive are the answers? I wonder.

"It depends upon the difficulty in arriving at them," the gray-haired clerk tells me, as though he'd read my mind. "I did indeed, young man," he adds. "I am Mr. Nicholas."

"I'm Fitz, short for Fitzgerald," I tell him. "Fitzgerald McGuirk. I don't see the prices on anything, Mr. Nicholas," I say, approaching the counter.

"Much goes into arriving at the proper price, Fitzgerald," the old man replies, looking down his glasses at me. "Do you intend to trade the clothes you are wearing for another outfit?"

I look at myself in the full-length mirror, liking what I see but tired of what I see at the same time. My Levi's and leather jacket have won me many chums but, so far, no lover.

"Yes, a trade-in," I tell him. "By the way, Madame Ana said to mention her name."

"Madame Ana sends us a good many of our customers."

Mr. Nicholas steps from behind the counter and circles me, looking me up and down. It makes me nervous and slightly dizzy. He jots notes in his lined receipt pad with a pencil. The pencil is short, but the eraser appears unused.

"I don't suppose the duds I'm wearing are worth much, huh?"

He continues taking notes and looks up at me when he circles round to the front again.

"Not necessarily, young man. We live in an impolite age in which slovenly appearance is considered a virtue. Forgive my outspokenness, Fitzgerald. I try to be accurate in my assessments. They affect the price. And in what outfit might you be interested?"

"Oh, I don't think I could afford it, even with a good price for the gear I've got on."

"The formal afternoon dress?" Mr. Nicholas asks.

"Yes. How did you know?"

"In my business, it pays to know what your customers want. I have had well over one-hundred years' practice reading faces. The fresher the face, the easier it is to read: fewer wrinkles getting in the way."

"I don't believe you."

"That is your choice, young man."

He goes to the rack with the black cutaway coat, walking with a hobble, and lays the suit of clothes on the counter.

"Let me look up my notes on these clothes."

Mr. Nicholas opens a wooden box in which there are index cards. He checks the number on the white tag attached to the sleeve of the formal jacket. He reads.

"Ah, yes. A Russian fellow, classically trained pianist, around your age I'm guessing, born in Odessa. Can you read music?"

I shake my head.

"Well, no matter. You will assume his identity and have his skills, but it will still be you inside. You'll merely be putting on a suit of clothes. As the saying goes..." he remarks, pointing to the framed embroidered motto on the wall behind him. *Das Kleid macht den Mann.*

"I don't understand."

"It's German. I had my first tailor's shop in Buttenheim. It says, *Clothes make the man*."

"I'm hoping they do," I tell him.

He marks more things down in his receipt book and turns the cranks of his calculator.

"The formal outfit you selected includes the gray-and-black striped trousers, white dress shirt, gray piqué waistcoat, and black calfskin shoes. Your trade-in items are more valuable as it turns out. I'll have to throw in the silver cufflinks to effect an even trade."

"Really, Mr. Nicholas? That's great. I wasn't expecting that."

He attaches a white string-tag to the cuff zipper of my leather jacket. He asks whether I intend to include the rainbow flag pin on the lapel.

"Sure. Why not?" I tell him. "Maybe it'll bring the next guy better luck than I've had."

Mr. Nicholas grins, bringing several wrinkles out of retirement. He asks my nationality, occupation, age, and birthplace, jotting my answers down on an index card.

"I'm an American now, a theater set carpenter, twenty-eight, born in County Antrim, Northern Ireland."

"Thank you. Just so the next fellow will know what he's getting into," he explains.

I smile at his wordplay. He leads me to the dressing room and helps me out of my leather jacket and jean jacket, putting them on wooden hangers. Mr. Nicholas takes them away as I tug off my boots and step out of my Levi's. I wonder what I should do about my underwear.

"Your underclothes are your own," he tells me, standing on the other side of the heavy curtain to the dressing room. "We are interested only in appearances, the part shown to the world. Perhaps you will want a white undershirt so your black T-shirt does not show through your white dress shirt," he suggests.

I take off my T-shirt. He hands the gray striped trousers to me, reaching around the curtain. They are a good fit and far less rough than the heavy denim I've been used to for so long. Next comes the white undershirt and dress shirt. I step from behind the curtain. There are no buttons on the cuffs. The long sleeves would fit an orangutan.

"They are French cuffs," Mr. Nicholas explains, "secured with the silver cufflinks. Let me help you, if I may."

He folds the cuffs and attaches the ornate cufflinks. I cannot imagine getting dressed in this outfit by myself.

"You will get accustomed to it the more you wear these clothes, young man. Don't be daunted by your first experience of dressing smartly. Here are the shoes, Fitzgerald."

They are spit-polished and also a perfect fit. Next comes the black bow tie which he slips around the shirt collar. He stands on a short stool and, reaching around me from behind, knots the tie as though it were a trick of legerdemain. Then comes the gray waistcoat which he informs me is pronounced "wess´kut." I button it down the front and think of Henry Thoreau's advice cautioning against any enterprise that requires a new suit of clothes.

"You are free to Thoreau out any counsel that does not suit you," he says, chuckling at his pun. "Here. Let's see how you look."

He leads me out to the shop and has me stand before the large mirror, tilting and adjusting it on its stand until all of me appears within its oval frame.

"What's going on?" I say. "That's not me in the mirror. Who is it? This is very strange."

"You are seeing the young Russian fellow of whom I spoke. You are wearing his clothes so you have also put on his appearance and aspect. It will take some getting used to, but you are quite unchanged on the inside."

He takes the black cutaway coat from its hanger and, giving it a shake, holds it out for me to slide my arms into it. Then he comes around the front and, pulling the lapels together, buttons the single button at the waist. He steps aside. I move my arms and turn my head in the mirror. I stick out my tongue and wink to be sure it is me. *Yes, it is me.*

"Whom else did you expect, young man?"

"I don't know. But I don't think I will ever get used to someone else staring back at me from the mirror."

I look myself up and down, squinting, admiring myself, liking what I see. Each detail is perfect. It is indeed an improvement. If this doesn't land me a boyfriend, I'm clueless what to try next.

"What do you think, Fitzgerald McGuirk?"

"It is hard to believe all I did was change clothes. My transformation is incredible, Mr. Nicholas. I even feel different."

"Very good, sir. Then you won't mind signing the voucher, the receipt."

"No, of course not. I'm completely satisfied. I can't believe it."

The odd little fellow removes the cap from his tortoiseshell pen and hands it to me. The nib scrapes across the paper like a skater's blade on fresh ice. He countersigns the receipt and its copy. Folding one in thirds, he hands it to me.

"You look quite handsome, Mr. McGuirk. Not that you were not handsome before, but your new appearance is more to my taste. I know you will be happy."

Mr. Nicholas leads me to the front door of his shop, putting his hand on my shoulder. I open the door, but turn on my heels—much easier in proper shoes than heavy boots. I'd meant to ask him what happens when I get undressed.

"You will naturally revert to your usual aspect, Mr. McGuirk. Beneath our clothes, we are all naked. That is when we are most ourselves. You will be yourself."

"Yes, of course. Thank you, Mr. Nicholas."

He extends his hand and I shake it. He has a powerful grip for an old codger. Oops. I forgot he's on my wavelength. *Beg your pardon, old chap*, I think.

Quite all right, he beams back at me.

I am drawn to look at my reflection in every shop window and doorway along Thirteenth Street. For the first time in five years, since I came to New York, the grimy and litter-strewn streets appall me. I used to blend in, but now I stick out.

Astride my motorcycle, I look ridiculous in my formal attire. I can't wait to get home and lay my good clothes aside, keeping them unsullied until I'm ready to meet my dream man.

Mr. Nicholas closes the book he's been reading and picks up the heavy receiver of his old-style telephone. He dials Madame Ana's number.

"Hello, Madame Ana. This is Mr. Nicholas."

"I was expecting your call. It's good to hear from you."

"I've finished the Richard Feynman book you recommended. I admit I remain a bit confused, but he makes a good case for traveling backwards and forwards in time, and for two things occurring simultaneously in the same place. It's rather like magic, don't you think?"

"I am glad you enjoyed it. Herr Einstein referred to it as 'spooky action at a distance.' Remember when you used to be his tailor?"

"I do indeed, Madame Ana. But Mr. Feynman does a better job of explaining these strange ideas. I'm just relieved to know that all the things you and I have been doing these past many years are not impossible. I've never felt comfortable doing impossible things."

"It never bothers me, but I am glad your mind has been eased. I wish you continued good fortune with your investigations, Mr. Nicholas."

"Thank you, Madame Ana. I wish you well, too. Goodbye."

Mr. Nicholas replaces the receiver and gazes out his shop window, wondering which one among the stream of passersby might be his next customer.

There it is: *The Vicarious Vicar*. The name must be a pun or some sort of wordplay. I don't understand most American puns because it is not easy to make a pun in Russian. I take the slip of paper Madame Ana gave me out of my pocket and check the number above the door.

I look at myself in the shop window, wondering whether I wish to go through with this. In my formal dress, I look out of

place, but, fortunately, it is still daylight. I thought I was being followed by two women when I emerged from the subway at Fourteenth Street. They wore too much makeup. Their clothes were
too tight and mismatched. My grandmother would call them
schmarovniks—streetsweepers, whether or not they were. Unfortu-
nately, they seem to be the sort of young women my formal attire
attracts.

I came immediately after my performance at the Juilliard
recital hall: a small crowd of mostly old men and their wives, who
wear too much perfume. But not a single young woman.

My dark blond hair curls around my ears. I am sorely in
need of a haircut. After removing my wire-rim glasses, I enter the
small shop, *A Fine Men's Vintage Clothier* as the lettering on the
door announces. A bell on a coiled spring above the door jingles.

"Good afternoon, sir," a crackly voice behind me says, startling me. "I am Mr. Nicholas."

"I am Maxim Andreyevich. I'm Russian—from Odessa—a
classically-trained pianist."

The fellow seems ancient, but he is very smartly dressed in
an old-fashioned way. In my black cutaway coat and bow tie, my
attire seems just as mismatched to this rude, crude age.

My sister tells me I have to be a little bit scruffy if I'm going
to catch the eye of an attractive American woman. So I am ready
to become a little rough around the edges, a little less refined, at
least in my appearance. I have pictures my sister Nina clipped out
of American magazines folded in my trouser pocket. It makes me
nervous to think of changing my appearance, but I am desperate.

"Yes, I understand completely," the old fellow says, though
I hadn't said a word to him. "This way, if you please, Mr. Andreyevich. Pardon me a moment," he says, taking an index card
from a small wooden box on the shop counter. "And what is your
age, if you don't mind?"

"I am twenty-eight, Mr. Nicholas. I began my musical edu-
cation at age six, with Boris Kirin."

"That is quite impressive, Mr. Andreyevich."

He leans over the counter and scribbles a few lines on the
card and returns it to the box, leaving a corner sticking up. I con-

tinue following him up and down the narrow, but neatly arranged aisles.

"Here we are."

We stand before a motorcycle rider's outfit of a black leather jacket and blue jeans. Beneath them, on the floor, are black leather boots with buckles. It is exactly what my sister showed me in the photos. I turn to the old fellow, wondering how he knew what I was looking for. I reach inside my trouser pocket. The folded magazine clippings are still there.

"It is unfortunate when we must lower our standards merely to get on in life, is it not, young man?" Mr. Nicholas remarks.

He takes the items from the rack and I follow him back to the long wooden counter.

"I was sent by Madame Ana," I tell him. "She... uh..."

"Yes, I know. She is quite an adept reader, don't you think?"

Mr. Nicholas removes the white tag on a string attached to the sleeve of the leather jacket. He writes the number on the index card and places it behind a tab in the wood box.

"This way to the dressing room, Mr. Andreyevich."

He leads me behind the front desk to a small curtained enclosure, putting the blue jeans, jean jacket, and leather jacket on a coat-tree. Then he helps me out of my cutaway coat and waistcoat, draping them carefully over wooden hangers. I take off my calfskin shoes and gray striped trousers behind the thick curtain and pass them to Mr. Nicholas.

My music teachers back in what was then still the Soviet Union denigrated anything American. Blue jeans and rock music fought for first place on their lists of things to be roundly condemned and assiduously avoided.

These blue jeans are thicker and heavier than any I've worn, but they fit me so well there is no room for them to rub and chafe me. The boots feel comfortably broken-in by their previous owner. I remove my black bow-tie and white shirt, and place them on the vacant hooks. Then I slip on the black T-shirt and blue-jean jacket, feeling a completely different person. The clothes make me feel sexy and masculine in a way my formal attire did not. It is all very strange.

Waiting on the other side of the burgundy curtain is the old man, holding the leather jacket open for me to slip into it. I am getting a little bit stiff inside the blue jeans in anticipation of donning the black leather motorcycle jacket.

"Let's have a look, shall we?" Mr. Nicholas says, leading me to the large oval mirror.

He tilts and adjusts it so that I can see who I've become. A strange face, a rugged, sun-tanned face, stares back at me, registering my surprise. Like me, he has gone a bit too long between haircuts, but his unkempt black hair suits these clothes. I run my fingers through the thick, wavy locks.

"What do you think, young man? Was this what you had in mind?"

As the old shopkeeper holds my dress trousers folded over his arm, the photos my sister gave me fall from the pocket and flutter to the floor. I bend over and pick up the clippings of men in motorcycle jackets and blue jeans..

"I'm ashamed to admit it, Mr. Nicholas, but, yes, this is the look I was hoping for."

I show him one of the photos. He glances down and adjusts his glasses.

"Quite a remarkable similarity, Mr. Andreyevich."

"Please. I think you can now call me Max. 'Mr. Andreyevich' is put up on hangers for the time being."

Mr. Nicholas smiles and puts my "old" clothes on the counter. I turn around to look at my backside in the mirror. *Not bad*, I think. *No one will recognize me.*

"You'd be surprised, Max. When you least expect it someone knows who you are—at least that's what my customers tell me."

"Are you a mind-reader, Mr. Nicholas?"

"I am not so much *reading*, Max, as merely *listening*. There are thoughts in the air all around us. I can't help but hear them. It is much harder to tune them out."

"I hear music all around me, too," I say. "It makes it hard to concentrate sometimes."

"Yes. That's a good analogy, Max."

"What does that sign up there say, Mr. Nicholas? Is it German?"

"Yes, Max. I had my first shop in a small town in Bavaria. It says, *Clothes make the man.*"

"I'm hoping they do. I'm tired of being what my sister calls a *nerd*. Am I permitted to know anything about the fellow whose clothes I am inhabiting?"

"Why, certainly, Max. Let's see."

Mr. Nicholas consults his wooden box of index cards, removing one and holding it close to his chest.

"He's a carpenter living in The Bronx, same age as you, born in County Antrim, Northern Ireland."

"And his name—just his first name?"

"I'm afraid that is not permitted, Max. I'm sure you understand."

"Yes, I suppose so," I tell him, reaching for my wallet. "Thank you for your help, Mr. Nicholas."

"It has been a pleasure, young man. Put your wallet away. I think we can say this has been an even trade. Please convey my regards to Madame Ana when next you see her."

"I will, Mr. Nicholas."

I leave The Vicarious Vicar and head toward the A train at 14th Street. I cannot refrain from glancing in the other shop windows at myself, or, I should say, at the fellow I've become. While it may be only the higher heels of the leather biker boots, I look taller and straighter, my posture more erect, no longer hunched from leaning over a keyboard for hours and days at a time. I dawdle, wanting every young woman I encounter to look me up and down and wish I were her boyfriend.

After my Rachmaninov recital at the Juilliard School, I go down to the locker room in the basement. I change into the Levi's and leather jacket I traded for my old black cutaway coat and gray striped trousers.

My changed appearance is not working out as I expected.

Instead of catching the eye of a fetching young woman, my outfit attracts young men. Their insistence that I "must be gay" both un-nerves and frustrates me. Where are the nice girls who like bad boys?

Heading south on Broadway, I walk to a strange little bar over on Ninth Avenue called The Ornery Burro. It's a tavern that seems to draw twice as many women as men, though I've not yet been successful in securing a date with any of them. At least I've had a few nice conversations and have handed my number out many times. But I never get a call. After tonight, if it doesn't work, I will be returning my "rebel" outfit to Mr. Nicholas and letting Madame Ana know I did not meet the woman of my dreams.

After work I change from my dirty Levi's, flannel work-shirt, and work-boots into my black cutaway coat. I head to a funky little bar over on Ninth Avenue named The Ornery Burro. After tonight, I think I'm packing it in. A couple guys there have caught my eye, but they never seem to return *my* gaze. I can't even get them into a worthwhile conversation.

The women, on the other hand, talk my ears off and are eager to tell me all about themselves. Often they buy me a drink. For the most part, they are quite smashing and intelligent. They give me their phone numbers at parting. I haven't the heart to tell them my clothes are a prop, a costume, and that I'd rather they jotted down their brothers' or their cousins' phone numbers.

I enter the pub and order an Old Curmudgeon whisky, sit-ting slightly sideways so I can keep an eye on the front door. I take the receipt from Mr. Nicholas from my waistcoat pocket and look over the terms of exchange. It's too bad things have not turned out as I'd hoped.

On my periphery, someone comes out of the men's room and takes the last stool at the end of the bar. I turn to look at him.

Holy crap. It's me—or, rather the guy who traded for my old boots and Levi's and leather jacket. I wonder, *What if this guy is gay? That'd be some coincidence, wouldn't it?*

He's still wearing my rainbow flag pin. He stands stock-still, his mouth agape.

"You've got my clothes on. You're me," he says, nearly out of breath.

"Hey, it was a fair trade. You're wearing my duds, dude. Makes us even," I tell him.

"Perhaps it does," he admits, breaking into a weak grin. "I'm Maxim Andreyevich."

"Fitzgerald McGuirk," I tell him. "What're you having?" I ask.

"Russian vodka on ice."

I signal to the bartender and order Maxim's drink. We shake hands and toast each other.

"Sláinte," I say.

"Za zdaróvye," he replies, raising his glass. "Please call me Max. Everyone does."

"Call me Fitz," I say. "Tell me, Max. Are you happy wearing my clothes?"

Max grimaces and takes a long swallow of his vodka.

"No, not actually," he replies. "I had hoped to attract a smart, good-looking woman, but the only people interested in me are gay men. I think I'm going to return my outfit... *your* outfit."

I nearly choke on my whisky. I do not want to laugh at him.

"Max, you're still wearing the rainbow flag pin. Don't you know what that means?"

"Well, like unicorns and little furry creatures, things that make women smile, showing my gentler side despite my rough and randy exterior."

"That's *rough and ready*, Max. The rainbow flag is a gay symbol. That's why you were reeling in men instead of women. Wrong bait, dude."

Though I try not to, I'm unable to keep from chuckling. Max twists my face into an expression of annoyance and displeasure. At last he surrenders to a weak smile.

"I fared no better wearing your stuff, you know," I tell him. "Can I buy you another?"

Max downs the rest of his vodka. I catch Lloyd the bartender's attention and order a second whisky and a vodka.

"What was wrong with my clothes?" Max asks.

"Nothing," I say, "except that I was trying to turn a good-looking guy's head, not a woman's, though I met some very nice women."

"You mean you're gay?" Max asks, nearly sputtering. "I'm wearing your clothes."

"Don't worry. None of it rubs off. You still like women and I still like men."

He nods and laughs.

"Shall we trade?" I suggest.

"Is there nothing in the agreement we signed with Mr. Nicholas to prohibit our exchange?"

"No, I checked it. We own the clothes we are wearing, free to do whatever we like with them."

"Then shall we exchange clothes, Fitz? In the bathroom?"

"OK," I say.

We leave our drinks on the bar and head for the men's room.

Max and I occupy adjoining stalls. We hang the items of each other's clothing over the divider. I nudge his shoes underneath it and he pushes my boots across to me. We emerge from the stalls at the same moment.

"That's much better," I say. "I feel like myself again. How about you, Max?"

"Yes, indeed. It was a foolish experiment, was it not?"

"I'm not so sure it was foolish. You found guys paying attention to you while you wore my Levi's. So why can't I?"

"And you attracted women wearing my cutaway coat, so what's wrong with me?"

We leave the restroom and return to the bar. Just as we are about to resume our places, my cousin Phaedre enters The Ornery Burro. Max stops. His eyes lock with Phaedre's.

"What're you doing here, Fitz?" she asks me.

"Probably the same thing as you, Cuz."

"Who is your friend?" she asks, her voice lilting.

"This is Maxim. He's just played at Juilliard. This is my

cousin, Phaedre McGuirk," I say, introducing them.

I don't think either Max or my cousin have blinked since they laid eyes on each other.

"So what brings you to The Ornery Burro, Phaedre?"

"I'm meeting an actor for a part at Circus McGuirkus. I guess you could say this will be his audition. But I'm early."

"Circus McGuirkus is Phaedre's little performance company," I tell Max. "It's our family name. I sometimes build her stage sets."

I move to my cousin's other side and let her take the stool next to Max. They shake hands and Max nods. I don't think they noticed I was no longer sitting between them.

The front door breezes open and a Mexican fellow in snug jeans, boots and a black T-shirt walks in, a jean jacket slung over his shoulder. His eyes are mesmerizing and his hair is as black as coal. He smiles at me and turns to my cousin.

"Phaedre McGuirk?"

"Yes," she replies. "Antonio?"

He nods while locking eyes with me again.

"Lloyd," I say, raising my hand. " A round all the way around."

The bartender nods and asks what Phaedre and Antonio are having. Phaedre is also having Old Curmudgeon and Max another vodka. Antonio orders a Dos Equis beer. He puts his jean jacket on and climbs onto the stool next to me.

"Aren't we a jolly bunch?" my cousin remarks.

Lloyd delivers our drinks and we introduce ourselves with some merriment.

""Sláinte, Cheers, Za zdaróvye, Salud," we toast in unison, laughing and nudging one another.

"*La ropa hace al hombre,*" I tell Antonio.

"*Clothes make the man,*" he replies.

"Well, certain clothes—and certain men," I remark, turning my smile on high.

———————⊃◦⊂———————

I doubt any of us expected to be at The Ornery Burro until closing We laughed and traded stories until we were hoarse. Phaedre and Max exchanged phone numbers, as did Antonio and I.

I felt a thrill as I tucked his number into the pocket of my Levi's. Strangely, I am certain he will call me. I look forward to getting to know him.

Antonio got the part in Phaedre's production of *Lysistrata in Reverse*, in which the men withhold their sexual favors from the women. I can't wait to see the play—and his performance in it.

———————————

That same evening, Mr. Nicholas picks up the receiver of his old Bakelite rotary telephone and dials Madame Ana's number from memory. She answers on the first ring, as though she's been waiting for the call. They exchange greetings, pleasantries, and gossip before getting down to business.

"It turned out wonderfully, Madame Ana, just as you predicted. You must teach me your secret."

He holds the phone away from his ear just as she laughs her high-pitched crone's cackle.

"There are no secrets, Mr. Nicholas—certainly not from you. It is question merely of reading people who will eagerly tell you who they are. You need only figure out what they want because, surely, they do not know it themselves."

He chuckles, but it is too low for Madame Ana to hear, even with her hearing-aid turned on. Her big floral turban muffles things, too.

"Perhaps I have a talent for spotting those who wish they were someone else, Nicholas, but it takes your talents to 'close the deal.' I could not do it, certainly."

"I am happy we spared them years of striving to be someone they are not," Nicholas says. "We saved two fine young men—though each in quite his own way."

"Not to mention all those around them who will be happier for their being happy," Ana reminds her old friend. "Shall we celebrate, my dear? How about the Russian Tea Room?"

"Too predictable, my dear Ana. Let's try the young people's place over on Ninth—The Ornery Burro, it's called."

"We will look painfully out of place."

"Not if we dress for the occasion. I am tempted to try the other set of Levi's and leather jacket I have on hand."

"All right, Nicky," Ana tells him, teasing. "I'll look for you. And I think I will slip into that sleek red dress you saw at my shop and commented upon so favorably. I shall wear that."

"Tomorrow at four o'clock then, my dear Ana. We'll have a jolly time. We will turn heads and give rise to comments and gossip."

"I'm looking forward to it. It has been a long time since we dressed up. Good night, Nicholas."

"Yes, it has been a very long while. Good night, Ana."

Mr. Nicholas puts down the receiver and walks among the racks of second-hand clothes, his hands behind his back. Madame Ana puts down the phone and walks over to the shiny red dress and strokes it with her fingertips, anticipating its cool silkiness on her skin.

Yes, we shall turn heads, they think simultaneously, as though still connected on the telephone.

THE PRISONER

Maxim's father, Cyril Andreyevich, languishes in prison for counterfeiting rubles during the last days of the Soviet Union. Maxim's grandmother, Ana, a crafty *babushka*, intends to get her son-in-law out of prison even though, after the collapse of the "Evil Empire" five years before, she has lived with her family in New York City. She has lost most of her contacts in the Old Country. She shares a sixth-floor apartment in Washington Heights with her daughter Moosha, granddaughter Nina, and grandson Maxim.

Ana conspires with her brother Nikolai to devise a recipe for walking through iron bars and thick stone walls. They send Cyril just a few words or a short phrase at a time so as to give nothing away. The prison censors and guards are more interested in looking at pictures of naked women with large breasts than in reading through uninteresting mail trying to determine, with ever-changing rules, what might constitute a breach of their supervisors' directives. They have more sympathy for the prisoners and allow most letters from family to pass. The guards, seeing nothing amiss in the brief notes from Ana and Nikolai, hand the letters to Cyril through the bars of his cell during their rounds. Having short memories that are easily distracted by the latest issue of *Devotchka*, they do not connect the dots nor realize the brief notes comprise a longer letter instructing Cyril how to evade them and escape.

One moonless night, I perform the completed recipe and simply walk out of Kresty (Crosses) Prison directly under the noses of the guards. I take only the bundle of letters and photos my family has sent me over the years, tucking them inside my jacket next to my heart to protect them from the cold drizzle.

After making my way to the outskirts of Petrograd, I climb onto the back of a truck bound for Odessa, covering myself with the tarpaulin.

My Uncle Nikolai has arranged for my employment on a fishing trawler on the Black Sea. From Odessa, I work aboard the old boat which is in no hurry to get anywhere. They are, after all, interested in large hauls of fish. I keep to myself aboard the smelly trawler.

At last we lay over in Istanbul. I have no intention of returning to the ship. A Jewish relief organization gives me fresh clothes, a counterfeited American passport, and American dollars. The money looks real to me, but the twenty-dollar notes may also be bogus. If I had my magnifier, I'd be able to tell.

The Jewish agency has arranged my next passage on a freighter bound for New York. I am not even Jewish. They asked only that I repay their gift once I am settled so that they may help other "prisoners of conscience" to attain freedom. I smile. It was not my conscience that landed me in Kresty Prison. It was my greed in forging large-denomination ruble notes. My friend Vladimir had cautioned me not to counterfeit anything larger than a ten-ruble note. In a hurry to get rich, I disregarded his advice. The rest is now, thankfully, history.

During my journey across the wide Atlantic aboard the neglected freighter, I dream nearly every night of walking down the ramp and stepping onto the rain-washed pier in the fog, all of New York City before me. I look up at the haloes and nimbuses of the lights and the streaks of traffic below the cloud-topped towers. That mist-shrouded scene is the only one of New York I have, depicted in every black-and-white *noir* movie I have ever seen.

That night, when I awaken, I see an envelope beneath the door of my tiny cabin. It is a long handwritten letter from Ana, my mother-in-law, and her brother, Uncle Nikolai. I cannot imagine by what means it arrived. More than half the waves of the Atlantic Ocean still lie before us. I have learned not to peer too closely into anything my wife's mother does. Ana always keeps her promises. That is enough for me. I do not care how she accomplishes them.

It has been more than ten years since my imprisonment and five years since my family moved to America. I miss my family so much—well, most of it. I miss my children Max and Nina the most, their mother less so. My mother-in-law tells me Moosha continues to manage everyone's life. When she is not being meddlesome, she is merely bossy.

From my mother-in-law's letter, I learn my son Maxim has given up years of his classical music training to take up jazz. His mother disapproves. Max has fallen deeply in love with a wacky red-haired woman from Ireland and followed her across America to New Mexico. Moosha does not approve of Max's girlfriend, either, nor her cousin, the one responsible for Max taking up jazz.

One of the other passengers has a creased and dirty map of America and I consult it. The way from New York to New Mexico seems as far as crossing another Atlantic.

I continue reading the letter. Max plays in a band with his girlfriend's homosexual cousin. My son makes me proud, plunging into the deep waters he's been told to avoid without a life-vest. His mother was against every change Max wanted to make. No doubt, when I was no longer there to mete out discipline, Moosha feared Max would become a delinquent, especially in a place like New York. But she clamped down too hard, in my opinion. She would never have let him spread his wings. I'm glad he has rebelled and moved far away from her interfering influence.

I did not worry about my daughter, Nina, when I could no longer watch over her. She emerged from the womb fighting and kicking, her shrill caterwauling still in my ears. I knew she would break as many rules as she encountered, a true *ikonoborets*—an image-breaker, an iconoclast.

Max had concerned me more. I was afraid his many years of rigid regimen in his classical training would drive the spirit out of him and replace it with repetition and numbing routine. But now I am not so worried. His girlfriend's cousin, Fitzgerald, introduced him to jazz and a rebel's attitude. I want to kiss Fitzgerald for that. He and Max call their band "Just Friends."

I hold my mother-in-law, Ana, and her brother, Nikolai, in the highest regard. They are much more to my liking. I find their simple ways and deep wisdom—to say nothing of their helpful magic—to coincide with my memories of my own parents.

I re-fold the letter and tuck it into my inside jacket pocket. I go up on deck to take in a little fresh air. It is a mild night, filled with stars.

Most nights I chose to stay awake and did my best to catch sleep during the daytime. It was not easy with the loud, rattling engine and the stream of announcements and instructions to the crew over the ship's loudspeakers. But it was worth my ragged sleep to behold the night sky mid-ocean from horizon to horizon, as though we were sailing upon a tiny ripple of the Milky Way. Night after night it gave me tingles up my spine, reminding me I was but a mote on an ocean of stars.

The night of our arrival in New York, my first time beholding it with my own eyes, I would not have known it except for the captain's address over the loudspeaker. I did not see the Statue of Liberty or the skyscrapers. I saw only fog and heard only waves lapping at the hull. When lights emerged from the pervasive shroud, I learned we'd pulled up at a pier in New Jersey.

Being in last class, I am among the last to disembark. I cannot see much beyond the grimy pavement a couple meters in front of me. I learn I am in Bayonne, New Jersey, with no idea how far that is from New York City. All my daydreams on the long voyage have been disappointed, but I choose to count the things for which I am grateful instead. I am a free man in a free country. What more could I want?

Out of the mist walks a figure holding a sign. The old man, slightly stooped, is dressed like a chauffeur. On the hand-lettered sign is my name, Andreyevich, written in Cyrillic letters. I recognize my wife's uncle, Ana's brother.

"Uncle Nikolai," I shout.

"I'm old, but I'm not deaf, Cyril."

We embrace each other, kissing each other on both cheeks.

Tears streak our faces. Uncle scrutinizes me up and down.

"You look good, Cyril. Come on. The meter's running. I'm supposed to be at work."

I put my canvas satchel on the back seat and sit down, sliding it across. Uncle shuts the door. It is a fancy car that smells of new leather.

"How did you know where and when my ship would be docking, Uncle? I didn't know it myself."

Uncle Nickolai looks at me in the review mirror.

"My sister told me. I never question what Ana tells me. She's never wrong."

I sit nervously on the edge of the seat. *How can Uncle Nikolai see where he's going in this pea soup?* I wonder.

"It's one of my little talents, Cyril," he says, clearly having read my mind. "I can drive with my eyes closed if I want to."

I see in the mirror he has both eyes clamped shut, just as he is negotiating a curved entrance ramp to the New Jersey Turnpike. Uncle is up to his old tricks. I try not to watch as he adjusts his fancy cap, tilting it first one way and then the other. He ought to keep his hands on the steering wheel. He is doing it for effect.

The fog grows even more dense as we exit the turnpike and get on another highway. I see from Uncle's dashboard clock that it is ten-thirty. I think the day is Thursday.

"Yes, you're right, Nephew," he replies, though I hadn't spoken a single word out loud. "You can't see it, but directly across the river is the island of Manhattan."

"I can't even see the river," I tell him. "Where do we get across?"

"Not far. We will take the George Washington Bridge."

At last I relax and sit back in the seat. Uncle Nikolai has his hands on the wheel. He hums to himself. I think it is Tchaikovsky.

"Right again," he says. "A piece that was never published."

"Then how do you know it?"

Uncle shifts his eyes from the road and smiles at me in the mirror. That is his answer.

We are on the approach road before the bridge comes into view. The New Jersey tower is lighted, but only the broadest details can be distinguished. Everything is a bluish-gray. The lights hanging from the looping cables and upright supports trail into the fog-shrouded distance, disappearing well before any vanishing point. The effect is eerie and it gives me a chill. I shudder. Uncle turns up the heater.

The Hudson River must be very wide. The bridge seems to go on and on.

"We are now in New York, Nephew. This is the halfway point."

I see the lighted New York tower looming ahead, red beacons at the top, and hear a fog horn from below. My first artwork in the New World has received its inspiration.

"That is good, Cyril. I can't wait to see it."

We leave the George Washington Bridge and, making a turn, are on Broadway, America's most famous street. It looks nothing like I imagined. Here, there is very little neon. The buildings have shops on the ground floor and five storeys of apartments above. We wind among the side-streets and Uncle Nikolai pulls over. On the corner is a Russian tea shop. It is still open.

"Here we are, my boy," Uncle says, climbing out and opening my door. "Your wife's apartment is on the sixth floor. I must return to work. Moosha works nights, you know."

I'm not terribly disappointed my wife will not be at home when I first arrive. I stand up, and my wife's uncle and I hug each other as an endless stream of traffic goes by.

"The city that is never awake," he remarks, though I think he has the expression wrong.

He winks at me and gets back in his black limousine. After sounding the horn twice, he pulls away and disappears into the fog.

I open the heavy entrance door with thick panes of beveled glass. Searching the directory, I find the right buzzer. My mother-in-law's voice squawks over the intercom.

"When I buzz you in, you must open the inside door, Cyril," she says.

I put my hand on the doorknob. A rasping electric buzzer sounds and I swing the door open. The lobby and elevator are sheathed in white and burgundy marble. The elevator has brass doors and fixtures, quite elegant, but nothing has been polished in some time. I push the button for the sixth floor.

When I get out, Ana stands at the door to the apartment waving me inside. Her smile takes up half her face. I am gladdened to see her, too. I never thought we'd lay eyes upon one another again.

She kisses me all over my face and swallows me up in her arms. Ana is sturdy peasant stock. I drop my bag on the floor.

"Cyril, Cyril," she repeats.

My daughter Nina emerges from the bedroom. She stands in an oversized T-shirt and leggings, trying to rub the sleep from her eyes. Her light brown hair is mussed. She runs to me and wraps her arms around me, squeezing harder than I expected. I last saw her on her eighth birthday, over ten years ago, when she only reached my waist.

"Papa, Papa," she squeals, kissing me as though she'd been saving it up.

"Back to bed, Nina. You have your test tomorrow. Did you put the book under your pillow?" Ana asks her.

"Yes, Grandma."

"Then you have nothing to worry about. You'll get an A. Good night, child."

"Good night, Grandma. Good night, Papa."

I am reluctant to let go of Nina's hand. It has been so long and now we must part again. My mother-in-law leads me by the elbow to the kitchen. Two places are set with bowls of steaming soup: dumplings in broth. The other bowls contain stewed beets under a spire of sour cream. She stands behind her chair and lowers her eyes.

"Thank you, Holy Lord, for bringing my son-in-law home to us. We are grateful for the food you set before us."

"Amen," I say, though I believe the Jews in Istanbul had more to do with my rescue and safe passage than their almighty, invisible God.

"We all had our parts to play, Cyril. Do not deny me my simple faith. There are many days I feel as you do, but I do not give in to it."

She passes the loaf of homemade black bread to me. I break off two chunks, handing one to her. That is her custom whenever a man is in the house. I dip it in the broth and fill my mouth.

"When do you think you will go visit Max? He asks after you every day."

"I would rather wait until he returns to New York, Mama Ana," I tell her. "I've done enough traveling."

"I don't think he wants to come back to New York, Cyril. He is with his girlfriend and his best friend out in New Mexico and he is happy. You must go visit him."

"Why, Mama Ana?"

I spoon the last of the soup into my mouth. I've been hungry for so long I do not believe I will ever be filled up. My mother-in-law ladles more soup and dumplings into my bowl from the still-simmering pot on the stove.

"Eat up, my boy," Ana tells me. "I have already set some of our supper aside for Moosha when she gets home from work."

"When is that? I do not think I can stay awake."

"She'll be home around dawn, Cyril. It's a good job. She works for the telephone company. But back to you son."

She refills her own bowl. Now that I have broken the loaf of bread, Ana is all right with breaking off more pieces. She hands the larger chunk to me, keeping the heel for herself.

"Your wife is opposed to Maxim's playing jazz, Cyril. She doesn't like his girlfriend and is against his friendship with her cousin. If Max comes back to New York, he's done for. Moosha will take control of his life again. She wants him to get a job at the telephone company. It will break his playful spirit, Cyril. It must not happen."

I sop up the last of my soup with the last of my bread and start in on the beet salad.

"What can I do, Mama Ana?"

"Remind him you love him, Cyril. Go visit him in New Mexico. Encourage him to stay there."

"In the desert?"

"You have not seen enough of the world to know that every place is beautiful, Cyril. A famous artist lived there: Georgia O'Keefe."

Ana clears the table and places the dishes in the sink. I tell her I have heard the artist's name but do not recall her work.

"Then you have not seen her work. Otherwise you'd re-member. You must look up her artwork at the library. Nina will help you. Come. You will sleep in Max's room."

My mother-in-law pulls the curtains aside. I think the room must have once been the dining room and connected to the living room. Maxim's grand piano occupies the entire room except for a small desk and chair in the corner. I see nowhere to sleep.

"Max slept on a little mattress underneath his Steinway. He never complained."

I accept her mild rebuke. After ten years of sleeping on metal bunks and cold stone floors, this will be like the penthouse of a New York hotel. Placing her hands on my ears, she tilts my head down to her and kisses me good-night.

"Good night, Mama Ana. Thank you for all you and Uncle Nikolai have done for me. I will go see Maxim. I have ten years to make up for."

"Yes, and ten years of my daughter's nagging that every-thing Max does is wrong. You must bring his life back into bal-ance. Good night, Cyril. My heart is joyful at seeing you again."

She smiles and draws the flowery curtains shut. The cur-tains on the other side of the room lead to the kitchen. They are already closed.

I turn out the ceiling light and stand at the window over-looking the George Washington Bridge. Only the nearest lights and the airplane beacons atop the closest tower have not been swallowed by the fog. It is a mystical scene, like one in a dream. I stand transfixed. I hear traffic below, but I can see only the streaks of their lights in the mist.

After laying my clothes over the chair, I unroll the thin mattress beneath Max's piano. I pull up the blanket and lay back on the pillow. Sleep overtakes me only a quarter of the way through my recollections of the day's adventures. I never thought I would reach this day or this place. My excitement over being in America at long last, reunited with my family, is no match for the countless sleepless nights I endured in prison. I fall asleep beneath Max's piano.

———————————

When I awaken the next morning, the full sun shines into the piano room, too brilliantly to see anything. There are no shadows on my first morning in America.

I crawl out from beneath Maxim's piano and peer tentatively between the dividing curtains to the living room. The window shades are pulled down, making the living room dark as a crypt. The hideous white sofa has been pulled out into a bed. I can make out a lump that must be Moosha.

My wife wears a turban around her head and a satin blindfold over her eyes. Though I do not see much of her face, she is still attractive. Moosha is snoring up a storm exactly as I remember her doing. I bend over and give her a peck on the cheek. She mumbles and rolls over.

I get dressed as quietly as I can, and part the curtains on the other side of Max's piano room leading into the kitchen. There is a samovar of tepid tea on the sink counter and a large crescent roll with a chunk of butter on a plate. There is a note from Nina vying for my bleary-eyed attention. I open it with the butter knife and read her note. It is a handmade card with a colored pencil drawing of the Odessa Gardens.

Dearest Papa,

You were still asleep when I looked in on you. Mama said not to disturb you, that I would see you tonight.

Until then...

All my love,
Nina

I drink the tea cold and tear the croissant apart with the hard butter. *No,* I tell myself, *no complaining in America. I am lucky not to be in the Kresty Prison cemetery.*

The clock on the kitchen wall says it is a few minutes before noon. I have slept nearly ten hours. It is no wonder I am foggy-headed. I shut my eyes a moment and think about what my mother-in-law told me the night before concerning Max. When I open them again, Uncle Nikolai stands in the doorway.

"I didn't hear you come in, Uncle."

"That's because I didn't come in. But here I am."

"Please, Uncle. My head hurts already. No tricks today."

"They're not tricks, Cyril. They're magic. It's what got you out of jail."

"I'm sorry. My head is spinning. I've only just arrived and your sister tells me I must go see Max. I do not want to travel any more. I am already here."

"Indeed you are. But Maxim needs you. You must go to him and convince him to stay in New Mexico. I will drive you, but I mustn't miss any more work."

I share my croissant with Uncle Nikolai and pour him a cup of tea. He sticks his finger in the cup, causing his tea to boil. He looks at me. I nod my head and he puts his finger in my tea.

"But isn't New Mexico two thousand miles from New York?"

"Much less," he says. "It's only one thousand nine hundred forty-nine miles."

We laugh.

"Come, Nephew," Nikolai says. "I will drive you to the library and then to Nina's school. Tonight we will have supper together as a family once more. There's a good Russian restaurant near your wife's work, The Princess Anastasia. Moosha will join us on her supper break. Then I'll drive you to New Mexico."

"But I will have no time to spend with Nina. I do not want to hurt her feelings, Uncle. I do not want her to be angry or disappointed with me."

"Nina is a big girl. She is eighteen. Her grandmother explained to her that Max needs his father's help. She will wait until you return. We won't be long in New Mexico. Come. Before Moosha wakes up. She has not forgiven you for getting arrested, Cyril. It will be best if you and Moosha get reacquainted in a crowd at the restaurant tonight," Uncle Nikolai remarks, laughing softly.

He opens the kitchen window and steps out onto the fire escape, motioning to me to follow him. The fire escape sways and lurches as we descend. It is like going down a rope ladder on a high sea. At the bottom, Uncle pushes a metal ladder on a track down to the ground and we climb the rest of the way down to the sidewalk. His leased limousine waits at the curb. He opens the door for me.

I have filled my head with the paintings of Georgia O'Keefe. They would not let me check books out without a library permit. I close my eyes and envision standing in the artist's landscapes in the last light of day, rose and gold outlining the mountains and mesas. Even the air seems suffused with light and color. Her style is at once so rich yet so simple that she approaches abstraction. I cannot wait to get to New Mexico and see it for myself.

Outside the library, at the curb, Nina leans against the fender of her great-uncle's limousine. She sets her school books on the hood and rushes up to me, throwing her arms around my neck and kissing me.

"Oh, Papa, I will miss you again so soon. But Grandma told me why you must go see Max. I will be patient until you get back. I know Max would do the same for me."

"You are a good girl, Nina. Your Mama and I may have our differences, but she raised you right. You are a very generous person—a young woman now."

"And also quite smart," she adds, putting her arm around my waist.

We get into Uncle's leased car. He closes the door and gets behind the wheel.

"We will go pick up my sister at the apartment and then take you all to The Princess Anastasia Restaurant."

"Is that the place way down on Ninth Avenue, Uncle?"

Nina asks. "I love that place."

"Yes, child. That's the one."

My mother-in-law waits at the curb wearing a frumpy dark blue dress, white sneakers, and a gaudy babushka. Grandma sits next to her granddaughter. With my mother-in-law now in the limousine, we speak only Russian, with many English words and expressions thrown in.

"Are we going to the restaurant now?" Ana asks.

Her brother, the chauffeur, nods.

"But it will be four hours before Moosha can join us," I say.

"Won't you and Nina have a little catching up to do?" Nikolai asks me. "The time will fly by like a flock of startled crows."

Nina rests her hand on top of mine. My hand looks so gnarled and weathered. Hers is smooth and slender and innocent. I am glad she does not wear fingernail polish.

"I want to be an artist like you, Papa."

I smile at my daughter. She makes me very proud.

"Judging by your pencil drawing on the note this morning, you have more than enough talent, Nina. And once I get back to New York, I will be able to help you."

"Will you teach me your shortcuts, Papa?"

"There are no shortcuts, Nina. An artist must draw every day, whenever you can steal a moment. And there is no shortcut to practice except more practice."

Nina pats my hand and leans to look out the window. Traffic flows faster than I would have expected with so many cars all hurrying, it seems, to the same place. Uncle Nikolai drives and drives and we pass still more buildings. I wonder if he is lost, driving in circles.

"No, I am not lost, Nephew," he tells me. "In fact we are here."

He appears at the curb, opening the door and giving his sister and grand-niece a hand getting out. The buildings in this part of the city look much older, a bit worn down and tired, more like a European city. Nina informs me the neighborhood is called Greenwich Village, but it has been a long time since it was a village.

The Princess Anastasia is a lively place with waiters and

busboys scurrying between the kitchen and the dining room. Our smartly-dressed waiter shows us to a table at the window and seats Mama Ana. It must be a place of honor. I sit down beside Nina and, just as a I look out the window, a young woman on the street makes eye contact with me and smiles.

I cannot help staring out the window, watching the people going up and down the street. I am not used to seeing more than one or two people at a time, usually only my cell-mate or a prison guard. There is so much variety among the passersby. It is hard to believe they are all Americans. I could draw them for hours—no two alike.

There is a lanky teenager with green hair streaking past on his skateboard. He nearly runs into an elderly black woman with a bun of white hair. She wags her finger at him and says something that looks like a reprimand. Remarkably, the boy turns around and, bowing to the woman, appears to offer an apology before racing off again, this time in the street rather than on the sidewalk.

Next comes an old couple in fancy evening dress, the man in a black evening coat and the woman in a sparkling red dress and fur stole. The woman latches onto his elbow and he steadies himself with his silver-handled walking stick. A girl and a boy, each about ten years old, weave in and out among the pedestrians on their bicycles. The boy's bike has training wheels and the girl easily outpaces him, though she totters dangerously near the curb at times. I see two men in jeans and sweaters trying to look inconspicuous about holding hands. They meet a gorgeous, auburn-haired young woman who gets between them, taking their elbows and laughing. The sidewalk is just wide enough for them to walk without uncoupling.

"Papa. You're not listening to me. Where are you?"

"I'm sorry," I tell Nina. "My head is outside. It has been so long since I had the chance to watch people who were not prisoners or refugees. I am happy to be here, happy to be with you, Nina. Please forgive my inattention."

One of the waiters draws the short velvet curtains across the windows. It is near sundown. My mother-in-law, seated at the head of the table, rests her hands in her lap. Her head bobs. There is a samovar and two baskets of bread on the table. I signal to the waiter.

"I would like a whisky, if you please," I tell him, "and a Pep-ski for the young lady. You may bring my mother-in-law a vodka when she returns from her travels abroad."

The young fellow smiles. "Will there be anything else?" he asks in Russian.

"Yes, some pickled herring and some caviar, please. There will be five of us—eventually. You may refill my glass whenever it is empty."

The waiter clicks his heels and departs.

"Papa, please don't drink too much."

"Dear Nina. You do not need to take your mother's place. Admire her industriousness, not her meddlesomeness."

I pat her hand. Her grandma awakens with a snort and quickly shifts her eyes, taking in the situation all at once. The wait-er sets our drinks before us, including my mother-in-law's vodka. He will deserve a large tip.

"Za zdaróvye," Ana toasts, raising her glass.

I swallow my whisky and Nina sips her soft drink. The waiter is at my elbow with another whisky as soon as I set the glass down. We spread the herring and caviar on little pieces of pumpernickel toast. I could make a meal of it.

Nina has brought her book-bag with her. She takes out her sketch pad and flips to the final pages. Her grandma leans forward and scrutinizes my expression. I try to give nothing away. One by one, I turn the pages. It is good drawing paper and she has used pencil and colored wax crayons. I sip my whisky to make it last, taking my time with each of her sketches. I become as lost among them as I was with the multi-colored pedestrians.

"Papa. You're crying. Are they not good?" Nina asks, her voice catching.

"No, dear child. Quite the opposite. They are marvelous. You seem to peer inside of your subjects, to their hearts. You must truly love people to do so many character studies and do them so well."

"What about you, Papa? Don't you like people?"

"Well, I used to. But I've turned a little bit sour on the damned human race."

"Cyril. Watch your tongue," Ana admonishes, smiling. "This is the New World. You must adopt a new attitude."

"I'm sure Nina has heard worse," I say, downing my whisky and knocking the glass on the table to summon attention.

The waiter is disconcertingly attentive. Both women roll their eyes.

"One more for Grandma," I say to the waiter.

I no sooner place my glass of whisky to my lips than my wife, Moosha, blusters into the restaurant, the waiters poised to fawn on her. She is dressed up in a flowered dress and a short-waisted black jacket, but wears a babushka. I set down my glass without taking a sip and get to my feet.

Moosha sees me and brushes aside the waiters. I wrap her in my arms, prepared to give her my best kiss, saved up for years. She is still quite attractive. I have not aged as well.

"Not here, Cyril. Not in public," she whispers audibly. "What are you thinking?"

"I'm thinking you're my wife and I haven't seen you in ten years. The public be damned."

"Cyril, behave yourself. See if you can set a good example for once."

Nina intervenes, leading her mother to the chair on her other side, thankfully, and not directly across from me. I hardly know what to say to her after all this time.

Uncle Nikolai walks in and takes the seat opposite my wife. Ana crosses herself and prays for all of us. I look forward to starting over with my wife. I do not want to be on Moosha's bad side.

It is ten o'clock. We order Stroganoff with egg noodles, borscht, and beet-and-onion salad. I will have a year's worth of beets at one sitting.

"Papa thinks my drawings are very good," Nina tells her mother. "He is going to help me when he gets back to New York."

"*Gets back?* Why? He's already here. Where's he going?" Moosha asks.

"He is leaving tonight to go see Maxim," my mother-in-law tells her. "I have already spoken to Max. It is important. He needs to see his father. End of discussion."

Ana is the only one who can silence my wife. I never learned the trick, the right spell. Ana bangs her empty vodka glass on the table and the waiter stands at her elbow with another. I swallow my whisky so he'll bring me one more and order one for Uncle Nikolai.

"Only one," Nikolai tells the waiter. "I have a lot of driving ahead of me tonight."

"Be serious, Uncle Nikolai," Moosha tells him. "You're not driving Cyril to New Mexico tonight. It's thousands of miles."

"Mostly just air," Uncle replies. "Won't take us long at all."

My wife pooh-poohs the idea and digs into her heaping plate of Stroganoff. I am surprised she has retained her slim figure. Before we are finished, she orders Viennese chocolate cake. I am already stuffed. With such meager rations as I was used to in prison, my stomach has shrunk.

"Papa, I have a book for you to bring to Max that he asked for. Please don't forget it," Nina tells me.

"Then why don't you give it to me now and we won't forget," I say.

She reaches down into her book-bag and hands it to me. While everyone finishes, Nina only picks at her dessert.

"That's the very book I tried to get from the prison library," I tell my daughter.

"Keep your voice down, Cyril," my wife tells me. "People will hear you."

I want to respond, but I know it will only lead to an argument.

"*The Magic of Kindness*," I read. "I asked for it, but the prison librarian told me, 'No, I'm afraid we no longer have that book. But we do have the author.'"

Uncle Nikolai is the only one who laughs.

"I must get back to work," my wife announces.

I stand and pull out her chair. I signal to the waiter for our check, hoping I have enough American dollars—real or counterfeit—in my wallet.

"It has been taken care of," Uncle Nikolai tells me. "The owner is a friend of mine."

At the front door, my wife takes my hand between hers and squeezes it. Looking around to make sure no one is watching, she kisses me on the mouth, peering into my eyes.

"Bring Maxim my love, Cyril. And tell him I would like to receive a letter. Have a good trip. Uncle Nikolai is a safe driver."

The family files out to the car. My wife takes the front seat. I hold the rear door open. Nina scoots to the middle of the seat and I help her grandmother to sit down beside her. I go around to the street and sit on her other side. Moosha instructs her uncle which way to turn.

The telephone company is not far. I get out of the car. Moosha and I hug each other at the curb and my wife gives me another surreptitious kiss.

"Let's see if we can start over, Moosha," I tell her. "The past is now so far away."

"That would be nice, Cyril," she says, smiling. "Please come back as soon as you can."

"I promise. Uncle assured me he knows a few shortcuts."

I watch her until the night guard has let her inside the imposing telephone building. Uncle heads back uptown.

Even taking the West Side Highway, it is a long drive uptown. Tonight, even with its towers unlit, the George Washington Bridge is impressively beautiful, a tracery of steel. The lights on the suspension cables are like a string of luminescent pearls.

Uncle turns at 181st Street. Nina taps my hand.

"We're here, Papa."

"I do not want to say good-bye again," I tell my daughter. "But I'll be back soon. I promise."

I help Grandma out on the other side and walk the women to the apartment building. Nina gives me a note for her brother. She swallows me up in a hug. I see them quickly inside, remarking to myself what a fine young woman my daughter is. Once they are inside the elevator, I walk back to the limousine.

It is impossible to see inside the windows of the car, as

though they have been whited out. The car is filled with thick smoke. Even opening the rear door and climbing inside does not dissipate it. It is the same smell I detected on my mother-in-law, especially in her graying hair.

"Sagebrush," Uncle Nikolai, says, "from New Mexico. My sister's favorite. It is the smell of where you will be going. You must keep that smell at the front of your mind."

I feel the car lurch and take a fast turn. The aromatic smoke is so dense, I can barely see Uncle. I don't understand how he knows where he's driving.

"I don't have to," he tells me. "I only know where we are going: to see your son. I don't need to know the route. I just need to know where Max is. He is our beacon."

"How does it work, Uncle?"

"I have no idea. I just repeat the magical recipe my sister gives me. The sagebrush is a part of it. I do everything exactly as she tells me and everything is fine. Your mother-in-law once told me that, so long as you do not try to go through walls or trees or mountains, most of what is between here and our destination is just air. Once you push those molecules out of the way, there's nothing much at all between here and there. Well, here we are, Nephew."

"You're kidding. Where?" I ask. "I don't see a thing."

Uncle turns the air conditioning on high and the smoke clears quickly, leaving only the strong, camphory smell of the sagebrush. I see a colorful neon sign ahead, too hazy and indistinct to make it out. Uncle opens my door and I get out, taking the book Nina has entrusted to me to give her brother. I tuck her note to Max inside it.

"Don't forget your hat," Uncle says.

"I don't have a hat."

"You do now. It's from Ana. The paisley kerchief, too."

He ties the kerchief around my neck in proper fashion and hands me the black felt cowboy hat. I put it on, feeling much taller. Uncle puts the lid of the trunk down. I like how I look in my reflection in the rear window.

The neon sign reads, *The Ornery Burro*. Uncle translates

into Russian. I laugh.

"Is there another kind?" I ask

"Your mother-in-law says to turn your collars up and keep the hat on until Max and his friend are done performing. It will be a surprise."

Uncle hugs me, making me drop my bag. He kisses my cheeks and slaps me on the back.

"Give my best to Max. I'll be back later."

I nod and bend over to pick up my canvas bag, nearly losing my cowboy hat. I push down the crown. When I turn around, I see only the red taillights of the limousine. Turning up my collars, I walk towards The Ornery Burro, sidestepping the many mud puddles. The air smells like it has just been washed by rain and lightning. Each puddle reflects a different color neon.

It is only ten o'clock—the same time it was when I left New York. There are different time zones in America as in Russia. The trip in Uncle's limousine took us no time at all.

I open the heavy pine door of the lounge and tavern. Sitting down at the last table in the lounge, I tilt the wide brim of my cowboy hat forward.

Max does not know I am coming. I did not know it myself until yesterday.

I have arrived during the musician's break. The cocktail waitress comes around. I order a whisky. The young woman has curly ringlets of blonde hair and wears a red pleated skirt.

She stops at the next table in front of me. They are a redheaded young woman and a brown-skinned young man whom I see only from the back. *He must be Mexican*, I think. *They might be Max's girlfriend and her cousin's boyfriend.*

"How are you both tonight?" the waitress asks them.

"Tired, Fanny. But an Old Curmudgeon ought to perk me up."

"You got it, Phaedre. How 'bout you, Antonio?"

I pull down on my hat, trying to duck behind it.

"I'll have another Dos Equis. Thanks," Antonio tells the waitress.

I see Max's friends from the side as they lean toward each

other, their faces illuminated by the single candle on the table between them. They are both handsome. Everything in America seems so fresh. I think of sketching them, but I have no paper and charcoal at hand.

The waitress returns with her tray of drinks.

"Here you go, sir," she says, setting down my whisky.

"Thank you," I tell her. "My name's Cyril. I'm visiting from New York," I say in a voice louder than necessary. "I know Max, the piano player."

The cocktail waitress smiles. Phaedre and Antonio jump to their feet and turn around.

"Cyril? Cyril Andreyevich?" Phaedre asks.

"That's me, ma'am," I say, affecting a Russian drawl. I touch the brim of my cowboy hat as I've seen done in countless black-and-white Westerns.

"I am Maxim's girlfriend, Phaedre McGuirk," she tells me, extending her hand. "And this is my cousin Fitz's partner, Antonio Morales."

I shake Antonio's hand, too.

"Welcome to America," Antonio says. "Why don't you join us at our table, Mr. Andreyevich?"

"I'd be honored," I say, taking my glass of whisky with me.

I clink Phaedre's glass with mine and tap Antonio's bottle of Mexican beer.

"Sláinte, Salud, Za zdaróvye," we say in unison, laughing.

I decide I like Max's friends. He's very fortunate. Phaedre is quite beautiful and her smile lights up her entire face. Antonio is a handsome mix of Spanish and Indian with hair so black it looks blue.

"We had no idea you'd be coming to Red Willow, Mr. Andreyevich," Phaedre says.

"I didn't know it myself. But here I am. I arrived in New York only last night."

"Did you fly out here?" Antonio asks.

"Practically," I reply.

The musicians come onto the low stage. The owner of The Ornery Burro introduces Max and Fitz as a two-man quartet who call themselves "Just Friends." I watch my son strut out onto the stage in tight blue jeans and a leather jacket. Phaedre's cousin wears jeans and a dark blue suit jacket. They both wear cowboy boots.

Max sits down at a well-tuned upright piano. His friend Fitz sits in the middle of an array of drums and gongs that he plays by hand. Max sets the jazzy theme, quietly at first. Fitz enters with his percussion, surreptitiously and imperceptibly. On the downbeat, Max slams out a couple of chords that Fitz imitates. They answer each other back and forth, at times smiling at each other as though sportively trying to trip each other up.

I am spellbound. It is music I have not heard before, yet it is familiar and friendly. Max's playing is urban and sophisticated, Fitz's rougher and less predictable. I am amazed at their unique sound and accomplished playing. I decide I like it.

As Fanny goes past, I stop her and ask her to bring the bottle of whisky to the table. I order another bottle of beer for Antonio.

Max and Fitz introduce their next piece and the place once more falls silent.

Maxim and Fitzgerald come to our table when they have finished playing for the night. Their drinks—a *Fonarnoye Toplivo* (Lantern Fuel) vodka and an Old Curmudgeon whisky—are waiting for them. Maxim eyes me, but I have on my cowboy hat and a paisley kerchief tied around my neck. He does not recognize me. *Perhaps the ten additional years are a better disguise than my hat*, I think. I stand up and extend my hand.

"Max," Phaedre says, "I'd like you to meet your father, Cyril Andreyevich."

"What? Can it be? I don't believe it," he says stuttering with excitement.

I take off my hat. Max folds his arms around me and kisses my cheeks. We stand eye-to-eye now. We are both crying. The words catch in my throat.

Phaedre, her cousin Fitz, and Antonio are also moist-eyed.

"Papa, I am so happy to see you. Oh, my God, I am so

happy. I didn't know you were even coming. When did you get here?"

"Only about an hour ago. Your great-uncle brought me in his limousine."

"From New York?" Phaedre asks. "You drove here?"

"No, Uncle Nikolai drove. I was just his passenger."

Everyone but Maxim laughs. He knows his grandma and her brother do strange things no one can quite explain. But they happen anyway.

"Where is Uncle Nikolai?" Max asks.

"He had to get back to work."

We raise our glasses and drink to our health in four languages.

"Thank you, Fitzgerald, for inspiring the rebel in Max," I tell my son's friend. "I'd always hoped Max would become an *ikonoborets*—an image-breaker."

Fitz smiles. He stands and turns to me.

"I am sorry to have to leave so soon, Mr. Andreyevich. Antonio and I are pretty tired and tomorrow is our day for chores at home. Good night, Cuz. Good night, Max."

Fitz and Antonio shake my hand and give Phaedre a kiss. They leave with their hands on each other's shoulder.

"Wait up," Phaedre shouts. "Can I bum a ride with you guys?"

"Sure. Back to the Sea Breeze?" Fitz asks.

"Yes," she says. "I'll see you later, Max. Good night, Mr. Andreyevich. I'm sure you and Max have a lot of catching up to do."

The group goes toward the front door. Phaedre turns around and blows a kiss to Max which he returns.

My son and I are now alone at the large table. The lounge patrons thin out. I grab the bottle of whisky, and Max and I take our drinks to the bar. We sit off to one side, keeping to ourselves. He does not stop smiling. I hand Max the book and note from Nina.

"What's this?" he asks. "*The Magic of Kindness*?"

"Your grandma recommends it. Nina bought it for you.

Uncle Nikolai brought me here and I brought the book. Everybody wants you to be happy, Max."

"I am happy, Papa: happier than I've ever been. I love Phaedre more than I can express. Her cousin is my best friend and we are developing quite a following, as you saw."

He finishes his "Lantern Fuel" vodka. Before he can order another, I pour a healthy dose of whisky into his glass. He looks over his wire-rim spectacles at me.

"You're out West now, Max. They drink whisky in these parts."

He smiles. I am so happy to see him again and to find him so happy.

"Your grandma says you will marry Phaedre," I tell him.

"But I have not proposed to her."

"Well? What are you waiting for?"

My son laughs. I'd forgotten about his deep dimples. No wonder he charmed Phaedre.

"Oh, Papa, I missed you so much. I didn't think I'd ever see you again."

He has finished his first whisky and I pour him another. One way or another I intend to extract a promise from him not to return to New York.

"You seem to have found yourself here, Max. New Mexico is a beautiful place."

"There are more opportunities for musicians in New York, Papa."

"And more opportunities for your mama to run your life. Stay here with Phaedre. She's the only woman you have to make happy."

Max pours himself another whisky and one for me.

"Maybe it is my fault," I say. "When I was sent to prison, your mama faced many more struggles and uncertainties. She wants to have certainty, Max, for herself and for you and Nina. But certainty is an illusion—like a trick of perspective. Because she likes her job at the telephone company, she thinks you and Nina both ought to apply to work there. I cannot rescue you and Nina at the same time from becoming prisoners to jobs you will hate."

He places his uncalloused hand on my gnarled knuckles and looks into my eyes.

"All right, Papa. I will stay here with Phaedre. I do not really want to go back to New York."

"Thank you, Max. I want to make things right with your mother, to offer her a little more security than she has enjoyed."

"You must visit us again, Papa—soon—to see New Mexico in the sunlight, in its full beauty and magic."

"I will, Max."

The front door creaks open and Uncle Nikolai walks in looking around. I wave. He comes toward us. Max gets up and hugs his great-uncle.

"Good to see you, Uncle Nikolai," Max tells him. "Please join us for a drink."

The bartender brings another glass. I pour him a small amount. Though I cannot read minds, I know what he will say.

"Just one," he says. "I have to get back to work. Za zdaróvye," he toasts.

Max and I raise our glasses. We swallow our whiskys, pay up, and tell the bartender good-night.

"Can you drop me back at the Sea Breeze Motel where Phaedre and I are staying, Uncle Nikolai?"

"Certainly, my boy. But I cannot come in. Please take Phaedre my best wishes. Your father and I have to be going."

Max and I get into Uncle's limousine. He drives the short way to the motel, its pink and turquoise neon sign resolving in the fog.

Max gets out and waves good night to us from the doorway of his room. Uncle Nikolai pulls out of the gravel parking lot. I ask him to please not drive so fast this time. He does not notice I'm smiling when I say it.

"I never know whether I'm driving too fast or not, Nephew. The speed limit signs go by too quickly for me to read them."

He winks at me in the rearview mirror. He shuts his eyes and leans back in the front seat.

"Just a short nap, Cyril," he tells me. "You needn't worry. I know where I'm going."

Uncle is a good driver. I decide there's no point in worrying.

I'm pleased that Max has decided to remain in New Mexico with his future wife. In her sleight-of-hand way, his grandma has arranged for his release from prison, too.

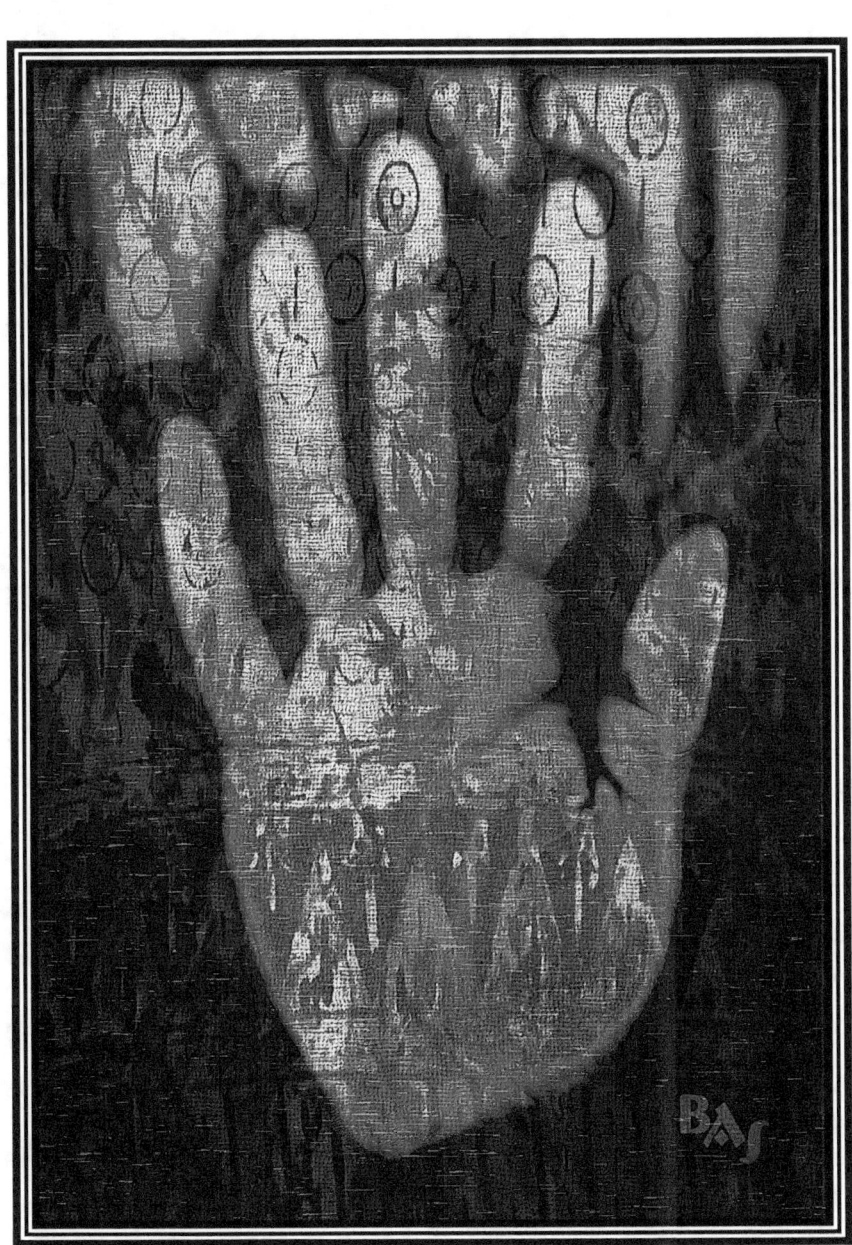

THE MAGIC OF KINDNESS

One of my few remaining memories of my parents concerns their teaching me about kindness. I, my mother and father, Catherine and Leon, and my brother, Nikolai, sit on a Turkish carpet in front of the fire. It is our house in Odessa. I am about eight years old; Nikolai would be thirteen. It is the year before the Tsar's police arrest our parents.

My mother hands be a baby rabbit that is all ears and feet. It wriggles and squirms in my lap. I feel its tiny heartbeat.

"We must always be kind, Ana," my mother tells me, "but especially to those smaller and weaker. Kindness works magic so powerful it cannot be resisted."

"May I keep *Mr. Rab-bit'*, Mama?"

"I think he pronounces it *Mr. Rab'-bit*, Ana.," my father says.

"He told me his name is *Mr. Rab-bit'*, Papa. I repeated it to him just to be sure."

"I see," he remarks, smiling. "Then I am pleased to welcome Mr. Rab-bit' into our family."

"You are responsible for him," my mother says, "for his food and cleanliness and exercise. He is not to have free roam of the house."

"But that cage looks like a little prison," I protest. "Please, Mama. If Mr. Rab-bit' stays ever at my side and only does his business outside, can we please not use the cage for now?"

My mother looks at my father. They exchange glances.

"All right, Ana. But you must keep his cage in your room and he must spend the night in his little house," my father says.

I want to object, but not a word escapes my mouth. I neither agree nor disagree, always the safest course when I cannot give them the answer they want to hear. Though he is older, Nikolai has yet to learn this lesson. He always says what he is thinking.

"The war has caused many shortages, child," my father reminds me. "I do not want you to become too attached to any animal we may have to place on the supper table."

"I won't, Papa," I say. "I just want to be Mr. Rab-bit´'s friend for the summer."

My parents smile at me and one another. I remember nothing else of our conversation.

My next memory dates to a half-year later. I do not recall a thing about my ninth birthday the month before. It is snowing. I smell pine boughs and baking bread.

My father tells me it is time to go out to the barn to say good-bye to Mr. Rab-bit´. I have dreaded this moment and wonder how I can save my pet from being consigned to the stew pot. We put on our lambskin caps and wool scarves and heavy coats. I stick out my tongue to taste the huge snowflakes. They taste like stale water.

"You remember what we discussed, Ana?" my father asks, taking my hand and heading into the barn. "If you are to provide for your own family when you are grown, you shall have to kill things to set food before them. It will never be easy, but it is better to have practice and do it quickly and with kindness."

"Yes, Papa, I remember. I wish to learn from you."

"You are a brave girl," he says. "It is not easy being an animal. You must never let them feel fear before the slaughter. That is cruel and will make the meat taste bad."

"Yes, Papa," I say, taking Mr. Rab-bit´ from the crook of my arm and placing him upon the thick wooden block inside the barn. I smile at him, then at my papa.

I had looked at my papa's book on animal husbandry, at the sketches on how to turn a bunny into meat for a rabbit stew. The drawings did not seem too frightful.

I ask my father if I might have a few minutes alone with my pet before saying good-bye to him.

"Of course, child. Call me when you are ready."

My father lights his pipe and goes outside. I smell the sweet tobacco and the cedar woodpile stacked high for winter. I pet Mr. Rab-bit′ and kiss his forehead. Then I call to my father. He sets his smoldering pipe in the crook of a log.

He rests his hand on my rabbit's back, stroking him gently. He smooths Mr. Rab-bit′'s ears back with his other hand. I notice the coarse hairs on his knuckles. He glances down at me.

"I will stay, Papa. Good-bye, Mr. Rab-bit′. Thank you for being my friend."

My father places his right hand on the rabbit's head and pats him. With a quick jerk, he snaps my bunny's neck. I hear the crack and my breath catches. I feel terrible for sacrificing the poor creature for our supper of Grandma's rabbit stew. Two fat tears escape and pat down onto the rabbit's thick fur. I look into Mr. Rab-bit′'s eyes, still open. He seems quite peaceful.

"The next part will not be so easy to watch," my Papa tells me, unsheathing his knife and stropping it on a leather strap attached to one of the barn's support beams.

He puts on a stained leather apron. After cutting a deep gash in the throat, he lets Mr. Rab-bit′'s head dangle over the edge of the wooden block, the blood draining into a bucket beside it. I think back to the illustrations in my papa's book. There was no blood, only outlines, and dotted lines for where cuts should be made.

First he cuts off all four feet and both ears. I think I am going to become sick. I hold my breath and look sideways.

My papa makes a long cut under the chin and around the head. Pulling the fur back, he tugs it down and over the front legs and down the body, like removing a tight glove. He severs the coat from the body at the anus. The inside-out pelt, requiring further scraping and cleaning, he places on top of the woodpile.

Grabbing hold of the hind legs, he slits open the belly from the rear end to its head. I cannot watch any longer and turn away, breathing in the frigid air in deep gulps so I do not get sick.

Papa places the bucket of entrails and pieces and blood just outside the barn door and summons the ever-hungry Vlad, our wolfhound, who devours it all.

My father breaks the thin skin of ice on the water barrel with the wooden bucket Vlad has emptied and licked clean. He fills it, washing his hands in the icy water. He tosses the bloody water onto the growing pile of snow beneath the eaves of the barn. Vlad eats the bloody slush.

I look away as Papa dismembers the carcass with a cleaver. He places what is now meat into the rinsed bucket. He closes up the barn and we go back to the kitchen.

He has saved one of my bunny's feet for me as a memento. *It certainly brought no luck to Mr. Rab-bit´*, I think, *and he had four of them.*

"Remember that the poor creatures on whom we depend for food must live outside in the cold and rain," he says. "They must hunt for their food and do not know how to cook it. It is a hard life, being an animal, Ana. Never forget that."

"Is it easier to be a human then, Papa?"

"No, it is more difficult, dear. We have no excuses for being unkind. We must always be mindful of what we are doing and how it affects others."

"Do animals not know what they are doing then?"

"You always get me with a question I cannot answer. You will have to ask your animal friends, Ana."

We shake the snow off our heads and shoulders and go inside. The windows are steamed up. There is a pot of dumplings roiling on the stove. My mother helps me off with my coat and hangs it on a peg by the door. I put my cap in the pocket that holds Mr. Rab-bit´'s foot.

"Poor child," my mother says to me, looking into the bucket of meat I have brought into the kitchen.

She stoops to look into my eyes. I see her concern in how she knits her eyebrows and wrinkles her nose. Papa holds his hands over the stove and rubs them together.

"It's all right, Mama. I am glad I befriended Mr. Rab-bit´. I will miss him."

My mother wipes my tears. She hugs me and stands up.

"Perhaps you should ask your grandmother how to make the stew, Ana. You need to learn her recipes. She is the one who taught me."

I have no appetite left, and wonder whether I will be able to eat supper.

Grandma is asleep beside the dying fire in the parlor, wrapped up to her chin in her favorite blanket. I move aside the brass fireplace screen resembling a peacock with his feathers fanned out. I stir the embers and add two logs. I catch Grandma peeking at me.

"Thank you, Ana. I was getting a bit chilled."

"Mama said you would teach me your recipe for rabbit stew, Grandma."

"Is your bunny now our supper?"

"Yes, Grandma."

"You are far braver than your brother. Come sit for a minute."

I sit down on the footstool for which Grandma made a sampler of the Odessa Gardens in full bloom. It is a comforting image to behold as the snow piles up outside.

"It is time I begin to teach you all my recipes, child. I will not be around forever. You need to follow them exactly as I give them to you."

"Yes, Grandma," I say, helping her up from her rocking chair.

"Thank you, Ana. My grandmother taught them to me."

I hand Grandma her walking stick and we go into the kitchen. She takes her white apron from the hook beside the stove and ties it around her waist.

"I lay out all the spices and special ingredients so I will not forget them later," she instructs me. "First, select five laurel leaves, three red mushrooms with white spots, and a small handful of peppercorns."

I realize her recipes do not involve scientific weights and measurements. A pinch is more than a dash, but just as inexact.

"Grandma?" I ask. "Shall I bring the sour cream from the larder?"

"Not yet, Ana. That is the last ingredient to go into the pot, to make the gravy taste better. You must be patient while things simmer. Next I'll show you how to cook the cabbage and beets."

The aromas of cooking revive my appetite. My father asks me to say the grace at table.

"Thank you, Lord, for the food you set before us, and to Mr. Rab-bit´ for giving himself so that we may eat. Amen."

My parents look at each other and smile. My father and my grandmother praise me to the skies, giving me credit for our meal. Papa calls me *precocious*, a word I had to look up in his thick dictionary.

My family and I enjoy a marvelous rabbit stew that evening. My brother, Nikolai, does not partake of the stew, eating only the boiled cabbage and stewed beets. He never eats rabbit stew, but tonight his empty bowl is full to the brim with envy.

———————⊃●⊂———————

When the hour had come, and I asked my father for a few final minutes with Mr. Rab-bit´, he smoked his pipe out in the falling snow. That's when I effected the substitution.

I found another rabbit that resembled Mr. Rab-bit´ in one of Uncle Nikolai's snares that was still alive. I kept the impostor in the wire cage intended for my pet, hiding it behind a stack of firewood at the back of the barn until the hour arrived. I never told anyone what I'd done.

My brother, who was named after our uncle, criticized me for sacrificing *any* rabbit to the stew pot. He said I should eat only lettuce like Mr. Rab-bit´. I think Nikolai's feelings are misdirected. He was not nearly as concerned about our own species, whose members the agents of the Tsar regularly line up against a wall to be shot or send them to Siberia, like our own parents. Some disappear mysteriously without a trace.

I enjoyed the real Mr. Rab-bit´'s company for another year,

after which his time on earth ran out and my pet died of old age. I buried him among the roots of my favorite tree, a towering oak whose wrinkled bark seemed to contain many strange faces, depending on which angle the daylight or moonlight shone across it.

I kept the foot of Mr. Rab-bit''s stand-in as a reminder of both my parents, of my mother's soft lessons and my father's hard ones. They have both made me who I am. I have the lucky rabbit's foot still, and I remember the lessons of kindness whenever I fondle it.

———————◦◦◦———————

Eighty-odd years later, I keep the counterfeit coney's foot in the pocket of my kitchen apron. I rub it for good luck whenever I attempt a new recipe—not a cooking recipe, but a formula for doing other things, magical things. Grandma called them spells or formulas or recipes depending on her mood. So long as they worked, I did not care what they were called.

At first I took all my grandma's recipes quite literally, word for word. It was many years before I learned her recipes were metaphors. They were how she turned one thing into another so effortlessly. One thing was not *like* another, requiring many words and wordy qualifications. Rather, one thing simply *became* another thing. All the magic I learned from her was that kind of metaphorical, phantasmagorical magic. The recipes never turned out quite the same way twice. Like her pinches and dashes, they were approximations, never meant to be understood literally.

"If you truly trust that a thing will happen, Ana, it happens," my grandma told me. "But doubt is a heavy stone that holds your intentions down. Your dreams never leave the ground. Remove the stone of doubt and you will float, my child."

———————◦◦◦———————

A year after their disappearance, my grandmother tried to float my parents, Catherine and Leon, out of their Siberian gulag. She repeated the recipe until her forehead broke into a sweat.

"I need to know where they are, my child, before I can get them out. I have to tell them when this will happen so they will be ready. I cannot do this, Ana. I have tried until I am weak. Please, dear one, do not push me any harder."

"Yes, Grandma. May I try?"

"You are so young, Ana, and so inexperienced, but there is nothing else I can think to do, dear child."

She unfolds a sheet of paper from her apron pocket. It is one of the few recipes she has written down and I have it still.

"Follow the recipe strictly. If you get it wrong, I'm not sure what will happen. They might get stuck between here and there."

The enigmatic words and peculiar phrases of her "Recipe for Relocation" barely seem Russian at first. I am discouraged, doubtful I will find their true meaning. They can be understood in so many different, often opposite, ways.

That is when I discover my first rule of magic. When a thing may be understood in multiple ways, choose the meaning that agrees best with your outlook. It is meaning that shapes our world, not the other way around.

After kissing Grandma good-night, I go up to my room. Lighting a candle on the mantle, I stir the embers in the grate before adding a scoop of coal. I carry the candle to the bed table and get into my heavy nightgown. The sheets are cold.

Almost asleep, I hear a wolf, and then a second answering him. I realize they are talking. In the Land between Awake and Dreaming, I can understand them. They are hungry, ravenously so. One of them thinks he smells a rabbit and sets off to find the warren. The other wolf answers, but receives no reply. The first wolf seems unwilling to share his whereabouts or the location of the warren whose scent he is tracking.

Animals can be selfish, I think, *just like people. If the wolves had worked together, they might be enjoying rabbit stew, rather than howling in the moonlight.*

It is about then that I pass over into the Land of Dreaming. My dreams are the mixed up lessons of everything I learned that day. I may forget what happens in the daylight, but I always remember my dreams.

I practice the Recipe for Relocation whenever Grandma is napping, going out to the barn and closing the door. I manage only to retrieve a bunch of rats, one at a time, which the ever-hungry Vlad is eager to dispatch.

There are rats in barns and cellars everywhere, but rats also inhabit prisons. I think I must be getting close to finding my parents. Expanding my attention to include adjoining prison cells, I manage to bring four sleeping prisoners into the barn whom I must quickly return before they awaken.

I do each of the prisoners a kindness by returning him a mile from where I found him.

After refusing to give up my search for my parents, I again recite the recipe. I accidentally relocate a sleeping prison guard to our barn.

The guard, whose chair did not make the journey with him, crashes onto the dirt floor of the barn on his rear end, jolting him rudely awake. On his uniform is the emblem of Their Majesties' Kresty (Crosses) Prison in St. Petersburg. I am as startled as the guard, but attempt to keep control of the situation. I have caught him off *his* guard.

I put a burlap sack around my head and shoulders, wearing it like Grandma wears her shawl. Darkening my face with ashes from the scuttle, I stand on two logs behind the wood pile so I appear taller. I disguise my voice, speaking as deeply as I can manage, and cackling like a crone.

"To your feet," I demand. "Any untoward moves and I shall send you back. You'll be sharing a bunk with those over whom you now stand guard."

The guard swallows hard. I watch his Adam's apple bob.

"If you please, do not harm me, good witch."

"Is that who you think I am, you superstitious fool? I am far more formidable than a mere witch. I am the daughter of Catherine and Leon Mendeleyev, and nothing is more powerful than love. What do you know of their plight? Speak."

The guard trembles.

"They were sent to Siberia two months ago. Their train was blown up and derailed by members of the Revolutionary Guard.

More than half the prisoners were killed."

"That's called liberating them, I suppose?" I snarl at him. "What about the Mendeleyevs?"

"I wouldn't know that, ma'am. Only the Superintendent would have the information on the accident."

"Then you'll have to get that information or the Superintendent will be receiving a very defamatory letter from me regarding your character. You'll be going back now. You have three days to look over the Mendeleyevs' records before I send for you again."

I close my eyes and invoke the recipe that sends Their Majesties' guard back to Kresty Prison. I am sweating despite its being below freezing in the barn.

I long to tell my grandma or my brother of my interaction with the Kresty Prison guard, but Grandma has been confined to her bed upon the doctor's orders. And Nikolai would likely not believe how I came by the information the guard imparted to me.

Disappointed, I go upstairs and confide my fears to the real Mr. Rab-bit´ who now shares my bedroom.

———————◦◦———————

This is the day I must again summon the guard from Kresty Prison, almost fifteen hundred kilometers from Odessa in St. Petersburg. My grandmother would be quite cross if she found out I have succeeded where she failed.

Certainly I do not think I am more skilled at magic than she is. After all, she is my teacher. I think she failed because she was not imaginative enough. She thought my mother and father were languishing in Siberia. That was the only place she looked for them. Instead, I sought my parents rather than their whereabouts. Their presence was last felt in St. Petersburg and that's where I looked for them.

It also helped, I think, that I had complete confidence when I confronted the guard. It is not the stone from David's sling that slew Goliath. It was David's confidence that he could hurl the stone in deadly fashion that cut the giant down. Confidence is the second rule of magic.

I close my eyes and seek out the guard. When I open them

again, the quivering guard stands before me, soup in his whiskers. I have taken pains to make my face as hideous as possible, again using coal and ashes.

"Well," I inquire, placing my hands on my hips and scowling. "What news have you to tell me?"

"Please, ma'am. I have done what you asked. The Superintendent's report states that the bodies of Catherine and Leon Mendeleyev were never recovered. They are missing. Please, send me back. I do not care for this place."

"Gladly. Only an utter fool would want to be sent back to prison. You are in prison even when you are not behind bars."

I shut my eyes and recite the recipe in reverse. Choosing to be kind to the guard, I transfer his supervisor's supper to his guard station. It is a beautiful slab of beef with boiled potatoes, all of it smothered in gravy. Of course, the guard will lose his position, but, when the Bolsheviks storm Kresty Prison in a fortnight, the guard will be miles away on his brother's farm, his life spared.

I open my eyes to find I am alone in the barn once again.

The news from the guard is not the best for which I'd hoped, but neither is it the worst. My parents have not been found, a fact that I interpret as their having escaped. That remains my position to this day, nearly eight decades later and two continents away. To this day, I have not lost hope—or my lucky rabbit's foot.

———————◦———————

Two years after my parents were taken away by the Tsar's police, my grandma died and the Revolution began. Both events made me very sad. There was so much I wanted to learn yet from Grandma. I was now entirely on my own.

My brother did not believe in magic. Nikolai believed only in pragmatism and the Revolution. There was already so much misery and cruelty in the world. I'd rather he believed in the power of kindness.

I had just turned eleven years old and my brother sixteen. We now lived alone in the house. He grew cross with me when I referred to his beloved Revolution as the "Retribution." In the end, my cynical viewpoint proved the more accurate version of history.

Nikolai was conscripted into the Red Army. I did not lay eyes on Nikolai again for nearly thirty years.

I catch an old man, wizened by hardship, stealing apples from my fruit and vegetable stall in the market square in Odessa. I nearly break his fingers. It is only four years since the Nazi invaders had been expelled from our Motherland.

"Just a pittance for a soldier and comrade," he says to me, pleading with his eyes.

I recognize my brother at once, but he does not seem to know who stands before him. His grim life is written in his face, though his eyes, his inner spark, still shine a dazzling blue.

"I don't know that one more theft will matter much, Nikolai Medeleyev, with the People's Commissariat closing in on you."

My brother turns to flee, but trips over a basket full of beets and sprawls into the street. I decide to have mercy on him, though I badly want to continue the prank.

"It is I, Nikolai: your sister."

"Ana," he exclaims, scrambling to his feet. "I thought you were dead. I have seen so much death and suffering."

"So have these eyes, Nikolai. We are lucky to be alive."

We hug and kiss and weep tears of joy, dancing around each other in the middle of the street, requiring passersby to maneuver around us.

"Come, Nikolai. Help me pack up my cart and hitch it to my mule, Comrade Stalin."

Nikolai laughs. His smile lights up his face, making years of woe and worry vanish.

"I can always count on you to make me laugh. It is wonderful medicine, Ana."

Nikolai's laughter leads to his coughing. He has trouble breathing.

"You will stay with me, Nikolai," I tell him. "I have a small divan in a small parlor in a small house. I shall make us a fine supper."

"And I have a bit of refreshment near my heart," he replies, patting the breast pocket of his dirty and frayed wool jacket, a souvenir of his days in the Red Army.

We walk beside Comrade Stalin. I swat his flanks when he balks. Nikolai and I are breathless, trying to fit thirty years of stories into a thirty-minute walk. We reach my little thatched house and put the produce, the cart, and the mule in the leaning barn.

We enter the kitchen, still holding hands, as though to ensure we do not lose one another again.

Nikolai is surprised to meet my daughter, Moosha, who is being cared for by a neighbor girl on the days that are too cold and blustery to let the one-year-old accompany me to the market square. My brother had not even known I was married. He makes faces at Moosha and tickles her chin. She spits on him.

The neighbor girl puts on her coat and goes home. My brother and I sit down to our supper of lentil soup and beet salad, and my homemade rye bread with plenty of butter.

"Don't eat so fast, Nikolai. You'll get sick."

"Where is your husband?" he asks.

"He's a casualty of the peace. The People's Commissariat came for him a week before I gave birth. I cannot locate him with magic and fear he might be dead. No one has any information on him, not even what charges are being brought."

"I wouldn't probe too deeply, Ana. Inquiry is often a crime in itself."

"Please, let's not ruin our supper with political talk. Did you ever get married, Nikolai?"

My brother shakes his head and asks for a second helping of soup. I tell him he must let the first bowl settle. Putting the little one in her cradle near the wood stove, I hum a lullaby to her until her eyelids flutter and close. Nikolai finishes his soup and bread. We retire to the parlor.

The occasion warrants a coal fire in the hearth. Nikolai removes his threadbare jacket and takes out his bottle of vodka from the inside pocket. The bottle is unopened. The label says it is lantern fuel. We laugh.

I retrieve two small glasses from the kitchen, the last two unbroken ones from our parents' kitchen—though one of them is cracked. We toast to one another's health.

"Life does not seem so bad at the moment, dear Ana, does it?"

"Compared to what? Murder and starvation and endless winters? Oh, I'm sorry, Nikolai. I've broken my own rule. No more politics this evening."

"It is a difficult subject to avoid," he says, refilling our glasses.

"One day we shall be free, Nikolai—in about forty years, if you can wait that long."

"Is this something you have seen?"

"Yes."

"Then I can wait, Ana, now that I have my family back. I have spent too much of my life hiding below ground in cellars and basements and air raid shelters, hiding from bombs and armies and secret police. So long as I know that one day I shall hold my head up, and there will be nothing between me and the sky, I can wait forever."

When my brother and I have had enough reminiscing and discussion and vodka, we say good-night. Nikolai curls up on the divan near the dying fire and I place my husband's wool army blanket doubled over him. I take little Moosha with me to the bedroom and let her snuggle between my breasts. I fall asleep imagining the new world she will live to see.

———◗◗◗———

My life, and my brother's life, over the four decades that followed, was, as they say here in New York, "no picnic." My husband was never heard from. I could not locate him with my recipes, a sign he might be dead. I never remarried and my brother never took a wife. With each other's help, Nikolai and I made it through a long string of difficult years. God, and the little bit of magic I know, pulled us the rest of the way to freedom and full stomachs.

I showed my brother some of what I'd learned to do over the years of our separation. His disparagement of my magic was not as vehement as it had been. He did not argue with the results, though. He was eager to learn any recipes I cared to teach him.

Since his nature was already melancholic, I spared Nikolai having to know anything more than he needed. The only part of my magical abilities he accepted without question was my peeking into the future. I was never wrong, but it was never more than the smallest peek. The hardest part was figuring out what the peek meant.

When my brother asked me whether we would always have to live in fear of the NKVD, the People's Commissariat for Internal Affairs, I told him that very soon it would be dissolved. He got so drunk that night in celebration that I wondered whether he would ever become sober again or remain drunk for the rest of his life. I did not tell him that the NKVD would simply undergo a change of letters, to the KGB, the Committee for State Security.

He asked me whether we would ever live in a country that was totally free instead of totalitarian. I told him truthfully that one day we would live in such a happy place. What I left unsaid was that it would not be Russia, but rather America.

And here we are, just one year after the collapse of the USSR: I, my daughter Moosha, my brother Nikolai, and my grandchildren Maxim and Nina. We are free at last and my heart overflows with gladness for all of us. God bless America.

———————— ⟫◦⟪ ————————

My brother comes over to our flat on Ft. Washington Avenue for tea before work at around five o'clock on the days he drives his black limousine. Nina is at the library or with her friends or in her room studying. She is at the top of her senior class.

Before Max moved out to New Mexico at the beginning of summer, he would have been in his piano room—the former dining room—practicing, but also giving a recital to his great-uncle and me over our tea. My daughter Moosha has left for work at the telephone company. It is the only time my brother and I have for private conversation. We are still trying to make up for our separation during the decades of revolutions and wars and purges.

The rap at the kitchen window of our sixth-floor apartment startles me. I am used to Nikolai climbing up the fire escape, but he is never early. I pull aside the ugly curtains Moosha bought at Woolworth's and open the window.

"Ana, Ana," he says, out of breath.

"I know what my name is. What are you so excited about?"

We sit down at the kitchen table and I pour our tea. Nikolai takes an envelope from the inside pocket of his uniform chauffeur's jacket. It makes him look like some petty Soviet official with more embroidered emblems than duties.

"I did it at long last, Ana. I received a letter from Max he won't send until next Monday."

"Are you sure? Do you remember how you did it?"

"No, I'm afraid not. I took liberties with your recipe and I don't quite remember."

My brother averts his gaze and takes a sip of his tea. He adds another cube of sugar.

"So what is his news, Nikolai?"

He first repeats the old saying of which he was always fond. "There's no Truth (*Pravda*) in the News (*Izvestia*) and no News in the Truth." Then he adds, "From what he writes, I think Max will be staying in New Mexico, at a safe remove from his mother's power of persuasion."

To celebrate, I retrieve the bottle of *Fonarnoye Toplivo* (Lantern Fuel) vodka from the kitchen cupboard. I fill our small glasses and pour in a splash of tea.

"Za zdaróvye," we toast to each other.

"May I see the letter, Nikolai?"

"Certainly," he replies, handing the two-page handwritten letter across to me.

I take a sip of my tea and close my eyes, keeping my hand on the letter.

I watch my grandson write the letter as though I were standing behind him, looking over his shoulder. Not knowing whether I weigh anything, I lightly touch him. Max turns around as though feeling it. I shall have to return the letter to him. Nikolai has not got that far in his abilities.

"Planet Earth to Ana," my brother says, jarring me back to the kitchen table.

"I gleaned from Max's letter what he did not say in words," I tell Nikolai. "Max is supremely happy. Never have I known someone with so much joy in his heart. It makes up for many miserable years to see my grandson so happy.

"Max loves Phaedre, his red-haired girlfriend, more than his own life, Nikolai. We must do something to help them see that they are meant to be husband and wife."

A pair of pigeons flutter onto the fire escape and we turn to watch them.

"I will certainly help you all I can. I'll do whatever you tell me to do, Ana."

My brother's smile lights up the dark corner of the kitchen. We finish our vodka tea. Nikolai declines a second because he must work driving his limousine car, but I pour half tea, half vodka in my glass. I fill his glass with just tea and he adds two sugar cubes.

"Phaedre's cousin, Fitzgerald, is fast becoming Max's best friend," I tell Nikolai. "It is his first real friend in America. Their jazz band is attracting many fans and followers. And Fitzgerald has met someone, too. We must do what we can to help them all."

Another pigeon joins the first pair and a second male joins him.

"Do you think they will all stay in New Mexico?" my brother asks.

"Yes, Nikolai, I believe that is what will happen. Max will get out from under his mother's influence and everything will be new again. They will all be happy living in New Mexico."

The flock of four pigeons takes off in a great flapping of wings.

"What will you do about Max's piano if he's not coming back to New York?"

"Luckily, Max lost interest in his classical training and took up jazz with Phaedre's cousin just in time. Nina has decided she wants to attend art school in Italy. It will be expensive, but it is her turn now. I will have to transform Max's Steinway into something else."

"Maybe it is time to change the piano back into our mama's jeweled necklace."

"Perhaps," I tell my brother. "Why don't you ask your friend Meyer Jaeger? He always seems to know which investment will be the next to rise. I haven't the patience for money."

My brother finishes his tea and stands up.

"I must go to work," he says.

"What would you think of visiting Max and Phaedre and hearing Max and Fitz play their jazz music?" I suggest to my brother.

"It's two thousand miles to New Mexico," Nikolai says. "I asked Nina to look it up for me at school."

"No, it's not quite that far. Door-to-door, it's only one thousand nine hundred and forty-nine miles, Nikolai."

We laugh and my brother kisses my cheek. He opens the kitchen window and steps out

"Don't worry, Nikolai. It is all going to work out—to everyone's happiness, even Moosha's."

"Yes, I believe you, Ana. Good night."

I watch him descend the fire escape to the next floor where he disappears from view. Closing the window, I draw the ugly Woolworth's curtains.

On the way to my bedroom, I pass Max's piano room and draw aside the curtains. The lights of the George Washington Bridge shine in the dark, highly polished wood of the Steinway A. I stroke the lid and smile.

"Thank you, old friend," I say.

I am grateful for my small part in helping others learn about the magic of kindness. Kindness is the third rule of magic. No recipe whose intention is cruel will ever work. Kindness is a gift that will last long after I and my mother's polished amber necklace are gone.

Pulling shut the long curtains, I finger the nearly hairless lucky rabbit's foot. Perhaps I have imagined it, but I feel my rabbit's foot give a little leap of delight inside my apron pocket.

THE WILD ONE

My first whole memory is of awakening in the night in my crib. I haul myself upright by the wooden bars and rails and stand looking at the moon through the curtainless window of my tiny bedroom. There is frost on the panes that looks like the ferns in our garden. The window sash cuts the pale light on the floor into squares.

I increase my grip on the wooden top-rail of my crib as I dance back and forth, watching the moon jump from one window pane to the next as I do so. The wood rail pulses, throbs as I know only living things do. I realize everything is alive: me, the crib, the moon, and the ghostly frost ferns.

A few years later I learned that the pulsing effect was my own blood coursing through my hands as my firm grip on the railing constricted the flow. There are undoubtedly places in the world where that is true. But in my world, that is not *all* there is to it. In my world, everything is simply alive—and everything is magical.

My second complete recollection involves my Grandma McGuirk, my father's mother, who suddenly appeared in the corner of the kitchen where I played, drumming on the pots with two wooden spoons. In her hand-knit slippers, Gran made no more noise than Mulligan, our cat. She startled me.

"Who were you just talking to, Fizzy?"

She was the only member of our household who did not call me Fitz—or Fitzgerald when I was in trouble. She is the one who taught me her magic spells which she called recipes.

"His name is Mr. Kattywampus, Gran."

"Oh. Is that spelled with a C or a K, Fiz?"

Grandma McGuirk was also my kindergarten teacher while Mom and Dad worked. I knew my ABCs forwards and widdershins.

"He spells it with a K."

"Then I believe I have met him. A tiny man with skin all brown and leathery, wrinkled like a walnut?"

"That's him," I exclaimed. "And he has a long, pointy white beard."

"Take my blessing to Mr. Kattywampus when next you see him, Fiz. Maybe he won't have to melt into air the next time I walk into a room."

"Yes, Gran."

I don't remember how much of our conversation my grandmother and I spoke aloud and how much we transmitted through the air like messages on the wireless. It was usually a bit of both, like our odd talk at the table with smatterings of both English and Gaelic. It was doubly odd because we lived in the North where only Catholics and the Old Ones spoke Gaelic.

The other thing I recalled about that day was the sunlight streaming through Grandma's lace curtains, the elongated swirls and arabesques cast onto the kitchen floor. Dust motes danced in the intricate shafts of light. No one else ever believed I saw and spoke to the Old Ones—only Gran—and later my cousin Phaedre.

<hr>

The third important event in my life—at least so far—occurred when I was seventeen going on eighteen. My cousin Phaedre's side of the McGuirks—our fathers are brothers—moved to New York five years before. She wrote me once a month and I responded less regularly. I saved her letters. I told no one except my pal Jimmy from school that as soon as I could fend for myself, I was moving to New York City, U.S. of A.

I missed Phaedre. Neither of us had siblings—a rarity in our neighborhood of the County Antrim town of Ballycastle. We were as close as sister and brother. I looked forward to her newsy letters, usually about recent trends in America or the British Isles. This time, after learning the proper recipe from Gran, I called Phaedre on the telephone even though we had only the phone, no wires or telephone service yet. The hardest part was making her phone ring from three thousand one hundred fifty-three nautical miles away. I needed to know exactly or Gran's recipe wouldn't work.

"It's going to be a terribly expensive phone call, Fitz," Phaedre remarked. "We'd better not stay on long."

"Don't worry, Cuz. I'm using one of Gran's recipes," I replied, though I knew she did not quite accept magic as real. "Besides, I got a summer position at O'Connor's Pharmacy running errands and deliveries. It's just a motor-scooter, not the Harley-Davidson motorcycle I've got my heart set on, but it's a start. I'm saving up for my journey to America."

"Good for you, Fitz. I think you were meant to be here. You'll love New York."

"Jimmy found work at Cullen's Garage. We've both got some money now. We're planning a trip to Belfast at the end of the summer."

"What do your mom and pop say about your trip to the big city?"

"I hope they'll ask if we had a good time. I don't intend telling them until Jimmy and I get back. It's easier to gain their forgiveness than their permission."

"You're the same old Fitz. Listen, Cuz. I saw this movie you are gonna fall in love with. It's called *The Wild One*. It came out in the U.S. fourteen years ago, but the fuddy-duddy British Film Board only just removed it from their banned list. You gotta go see it."

"Maybe it'll be playing in Belfast when we go there," I suggested.

"I hope so. How are you guys gonna get there? Where will you stay?"

"Jimmy's gonna borrow his uncle's car. We'll sleep in the car."

"Be careful, Fitz. Belfast's as much of an asylum as New York."

"We will, Phaedre. We watch out for each other."

"I guess we'd better say good-bye, Fitz. I don't want you to use up your whole paycheck on one phone call."

I'm disappointed she doesn't believe in the magic telephone I learned how to have conversations on.

"OK, Cuz," I tell her. "I'll let you know how it goes in Belfast."

I disconnect my thoughts and hang up the receiver.

"That was very good, Fizzy," my grandma says, appearing suddenly at my elbow.

"Please, Gran. I'd like a bit of privacy. I am an adult now."

"You are right, Fiz. Perhaps I should wear a bell like Mulligan. But you passed your lesson with good marks. Don't worry if you need the telephone as a prop. It is a good idea to appear to be talking on the telephone in case someone surprises you as I just did. Otherwise they will think you are daft talking to yourself."

We smile at each other.

"One other thing, Fiz. I know you will indeed travel to New York—and you will stay for a time before moving up to some place even newer."

I did not know exactly what my grandma meant. But I knew if I asked her, her answer would be even more elliptical and confusing. Everything she said made sense only when the time was exactly right.

"But Jimmy will not be going with you, Fiz. You will have a new best friend in America."

Her revelation made me sad. Jimmy and I have been best pals since we wore short pants. But I have learned that things have their season and that nothing lasts forever.

———————————◦◦◦———————————

Jimmy and I saw three screenings of *The Wild One* in one day at the newly-opened Queen's Film Theatre in Belfast. We each bought a pair of Levi's blue jeans at Anderson & McAuley's Department Store before returning home the next day. The jeans were as stiff as cardboard and they chafed and rubbed. But we considered it a sign of manliness to undergo great discomfort to prove we were not sissies. We could be as tough as Marlon Brando.

When Jimmy dropped me off in the yard of my white-washed house on Clare Road, my father stood behind the kitchen door, ready to pounce. I knew he was not going to be pleased.

"We only found out where you'd got off to when we went over to Jimmy's mum's," he said, glowering. "Your mother was frantic. This is the very last stunt you will pull while living under my roof. The next one will see you out on your ear."

"Yes, Pop," I told him.

"I hope you lads had a good time. Otherwise your being grounded for the rest of the summer will hardly have been worth it."

"Yes, Pop," I repeated.

I think my not arguing surprised him and knocked him off his guard. He opened two bottles of Harp lager, one for each of us. It was not the first time I'd tasted ale by a long shot, but it was the first time he offered me one when it was not a holiday or birthday.

I told my father about the movie Jimmy and I had seen and showed him the blue jeans I bought. They were still starchy. I wanted him to be enthused, but he did not care for "moving picture shows" and blue jeans were just another bit of America he'd managed to do without.

We sat down at the kitchen table. His icy blue eyes bored into me.

"Movies are all well and good while you're in the theater, Fitz," my father told me. "You can live in their world for a tiny bit of time. But when the lights go up, you must go back to the everyday world where blood and tears and sweat are not a makeup man's effects. It is no game, Fitzgerald. Life is deadly real."

I had no reply for what he told me. Of course movies were not real, but then, the gray everyday world wasn't quite real to me, either. I think I lived somewhere in what Gran called the *In Between*. Though I said nothing, I had no intention of spending the rest of the summer grounded, confined to the house when I was not at work. Since I was not yet adept at Gran's Recipe for Corporeal Duplication, I held my tongue and bided my time.

My next "telephone" conversation with Phaedre took place the following Saturday when, as rarely happened, I was in the house alone. Mom and Dad and Gran went to a wedding in Londonderry. I had to work through the weekend and could not go with them. I was not sorry.

"So what did you think of *The Wild One*, Fitz? Did you like it?" my cousin asked.

"It was fantastic, Phaedre. It was really cool."

"I can tell you're getting out in the world. What did you think of Belfast?"

"Kind of big, kinda scary—and crowded—but I liked it."

"That's what New York is like, Fitz, except that it's more vertical than spread out."

"Jimmy and I bought Levi's like Marlon Brando wore in the movie. I didn't have enough for the leather motorcycle jacket or the boots, but I'm saving up."

"You'd better save up to live in New York, too, Fitz. It's expensive. You have to let me know when you're coming so I can find you a position. Did you shrink your Levi's yet?"

"Shrink them? What do you mean?"

The front door bell rang. It was a rusty mechanical one that Jimmy kept ringing as though it were a fire alarm.

I told Phaedre and excused myself to let Jimmy in. I'd invited Jimmy to spend the night. He set his book bag on the kitchen table. It contained six bottles of dark Guinness ale packed in newspaper. I went back to the "telephone."

"Say *Hello* to Jimmy, Cuz," Phaedre told me. "To get back to what I was saying, you've got to wear your new Levi's in the hot bath and keep them on until they dry on you. That's what the guys in America do. They'll fit you like a glove and you'll look super sexy. You have to send me a picture of you and Jimmy in your Levi's."

Jimmy shouted something to her over my shoulder into the receiver. Phaedre didn't hear him because we weren't really on the telephone.

"My family's in Londonderry at our cousin Katy's wedding," I told her. "Jimmy and I are home alone tonight. We'll try soaking in our Levi's in the tub like you recommended."

"Well, you guys have fun. Don't do anything I wouldn't do, Fitz."

"That's exactly what we have in mind, Phaedre. Good-bye, Cuz. God be with you.""

Jimmy pried the caps off two of the bottles of Guinness and handed me one.

"*Jimmy, maybe better put some more beer on ice,*" I said.

He laughed, knowing I was quoting a line from the movie. I remembered more lines from *The Wild One* than I could recall from *Midsummer Night's Dream*.

"You gonna do it?" Jimmy asked, trying to imitate an American accent, but his brogue always poked through.

"Do what?" I asked.

"Wear your new blue jeans in the bath," he replied.

"If Phaedre tells me that's the custom in America, I believe her. She's not going to pull a prank on me."

"All right. Can I watch?"

"You're not gonna try it?"

"I'll watch."

Though Jimmy and I had snogged a couple times and wanked each other off, I got the idea he wasn't as into boys as I was.

We took our beers into the bathroom. Jimmy sat on the lid of the commode as I drew a bath as hot as I could stand. My father would have complained that I'd siphoned all the hot water in the neighborhood.

"Well, here goes," I told Jimmy, setting my bottle of Guinness on the hexagonal tile floor and stepping into the porcelain bathtub.

The water felt awfully hot. I shifted from foot to foot, splashing water onto the calves and shins of my new blue jeans. I became aware I was getting a stiffie in anticipation of sitting down in the water-filled tub. It didn't matter to me if Jimmy saw it.

When the water cooled off a bit, I slipped slowly down into the hot water. Jimmy stood up and looked down at me a minute. Then, turning his back, he took a leak and left the bathroom.

At first I kept my knees up, lowering my legs a little at a time until my new Levi's were completely soaked. I felt the denim shrink on my body, hugging my thighs and crotch. My stiffie grew obvious even through the thick denim. The bath water turned deep blue from the indigo dye. The slightest stirring made the wet denim rub against my cock, stroking my boner.

I grabbed my beer and lay back in the tub, closing my eyes. Rather than picturing Jimmy sitting at the opposite end of the bathtub, I imagined a brown-skinned man with hair so black it looked blue. Just as he smiled at me, my sperm shot into the crotch of my wet Levi's. It was the most intense orgasm I'd felt in my young life. It was one I never forgot.

The only other recollection from that night is that I'd gotten the drunkest I'd ever been. Jimmy fell asleep in my dad's easy chair. I stood before the electric fire to let my Levi's dry against my skin. It is a sensation I love to this day. I always baptize my new Levi's in the bath.

When my new jeans were dry enough, I climbed up to my room, unsteady on the stairway, but too drunk to care. I climbed into bed in my Levi's. As I reached to turn out the lamp on my bed table, I saw Mr. Kattywampus in the corner, puffing on his hand-carved pipe. The little fellow always seemed to appear at important moments in my life.

The pipe smoke was sweet, like the incense in church. It made me alternately giddy and sleepy. I couldn't tell whether I were awake or dreaming, deciding it didn't matter.

In the cloud of fragrant smoke, like fog rolling in from the sea, I pictured the brown-skinned man I'd seen at the moment I creamed my jeans in the bathtub. *Who was he?* I wondered. *Where was he?*

I heard a voice reply, half inside, half outside my dream: *I live up here in The Bronx. Come and visit, Fitz.* The voice lulled me to sleep, repeating the invitation. It was a deep and resonant voice like an announcer's on the wireless—the *radio.*

Mr. Kattywampus stepped from the smoke, smiling. Then he inhaled all the smoke back into his carved wood pipe. He put his finger into the bowl and sucked himself into his own pipe, thereby vanishing. I remembered nothing more.

I learned at the Ballycastle Free Library that The Bronx was one of New York City's five boroughs. I asked Phaedre about it the next time we spoke on the "telephone."

"The Bronx is a bit rough and tumble, but so are you, Fitz. You'll fit right in. There are Irish neighborhoods, too."

"That's what I want to leave behind, Cuz."

"I understand. But you'll always be Irish no matter where you live."

"I know, but I'd rather live among other kinds of people. It makes life more interesting."

I pace the room, carrying the disconnected telephone with me.

"I've been thinking, Phaedre. If I worked full-time at O'Connor's and dropped out of school, I could book passage in about two years' time. I'll have to postpone my dream, that's all. It makes sense not to buy my Harley-Davidson Ironhead Sportster until I come to America."

"And what color is your dream motorcycle?" my cousin asks.

Not realizing she's making fun of me, I tell her, "Black, with an S-shaped red, white, and blue stripe on the gas tank."

Chuckling, she says, "I think that's exactly what you ought to do, Fitz: save your money and come to America as soon as you can. There's no point in delaying the inevitable."

"Thank you, Phaedre. You know me and you know America. If you say we're a match, I absolutely trust you."

"You'll love it here, I promise. When you're ready to book your passage, I can scout for positions. There's always a call for carpenters."

"Thanks, Cuz. I'll keep you posted. Good night, then."

"Good night, Fitz. Thank you for the telephone call."

I continue pacing back and forth, muttering to myself.

I've known I wanted to become an American since I saw my first Western. America is at last within my reach. The only ingredient missing is money, a small obstacle to my immense determination.

———————◦○◦———————

It was easier convincing my parents of my intentions to go to America than I'd expected. My mother objected mildly. Then she suggested, since I was of an age to care for myself, that she wouldn't mind, in the meantime, if I cooked for myself when I couldn't join the family and washed my own clothes. I never let her touch my Levi's anyhow. I agreed, but I sensed there was more on her mind.

"You'll be awfully lonesome in America, Fitz. There'll be an ache in your heart for home."

"But I know Phaedre, Mum. She's going to find me a position and introduce me to her friends. I'll be fine. Don't you worry, especially not so far ahead of time."

She smiles at me and strokes my hair.

"Getting a little long, Fitz, don't you think? You'll be looking like one of those Mods or Rockers—whichever is which. I'll bet you won't be missing my advice so much, though."

"Probably not. But I will surely miss you, Mum," I say, hugging her.

Though I was certainly no great expense to him, my father supported anything that would get me out from under his roof. We locked horns a few times, as fathers and sons are prone to do, but I believe he wanted to encourage my independence. I knew he'd miss me as much as Mum.

"You know, Fitz, if you apprenticed to O'Riley, the carpenter and cabinetmaker, you'd make a lot more money than working for the chemist. For sure, it would be a lot more work, but you're not a lazy lad. Shall I mention your interest to O'Riley? He's in the pub every time I walk in."

"All right, Pop," I said. "It was a bit of a bore working at O'Connor's Pharmacy. I want to learn a trade. Phaedre tells me they need carpenters in America."

"They need carpenters everywhere, Fitz. Well, you've got time to think about your decision to go to America."

My life became numbingly boring. I was either working or sleeping. I was learning a valuable trade, but I rarely saw my parents or my pals.

The good news: I'd saved pots of money for my journey to America by living at home and working all the hours O'Riley cared to give me. I gave my mum a bit of my pay for the household. I bought a used black leather biker jacket and biker boots, like in *The Wild One*, from a bloke in Derry who got married because there was a baby on the way. He'd had to sell his Triumph motorcycle and had no further use for his gear. He kept his helmet, though, as a souvenir of his days as a motorcycle riding bachelor. I felt a little bit sad for him.

At least I was in no danger of getting a girl pregnant. The jacket from the Derry bloke was kind of scuffed, but shoe polish covered the marks. I got my second pair of Levi's shrink-to-fit blue jeans. I never wore that pair to work.

The bad news: there was no way I'd have enough money for my trip to New York in under two years.

Jimmy started dating a girl we knew from school, so that was the end of him and me wanking each other off. I had no time for anything except a night at the local pub every other Saturday. I rarely saw Jimmy.

I had my last "phone" conversation with Phaedre on the eve of my leaving for America. She told me not to pin too many hopes on life being a paradise in America. I said happiness was not a matter of where you lived, anyhow.

"It's an inside job," I told her. "You alone are obligated for your happiness."

"What about having someone to share your life with?" she asked.

"That's not something I even have time to think about these days, Cuz. Sure, it would be nice, but no one else is responsible for making me happy. Just me."

"Sounds kind of lonely, Fitz. Maybe you shouldn't have worked so hard."

"I'll know the right fellow when I meet him. I'm pretty sure he lives in America. I'll just have to put my dreams on hold a while and wait until I meet him."

"Did Mr. Kattywampus tell you that?"

"He did. He's never misdirected me."

"I wondered if you still saw Mr. Kattywampus or whether you'd outgrown him."

"Outgrown him?" I asked. "He's been my friend for as long as I remember."

"But sooner or later, Fitz, most of us leave behind our imaginary friends."

"Did our grandparents consider the Old Ones and the Little People imaginary? Do you think our ancestors were all daft?"

"No, I don't," she replied. "I'd like to meet Mr. Kattywampus one of these days."

"That you shall, Phaedre. He's agreed to come to America with me. I was afraid he'd have to remain in the Old Sod, unable to set foot in the New World."

My cousin remained silent. We chattered on for a while before hanging up. I was a bit disappointed that the person I loved most in the world did not quite believe I talked to one of the Old Ones. I regarded Phaedre as my sister.

That night I had a good cry. It felt like taking a hot bath on the inside. I felt refreshed and had another dream about the black-haired man I would meet in the rain.

The day of my departure from the Old Sod had at last arrived. My mother, happy the minute before, burst into tears in the kitchen. It took her a little while to compose herself.

"This day was always around the corner," she said. "Now it's here."

"We ran out of corners, I guess. I'll miss you, Mum," I told her.

"Maybe you and Phaedre will visit soon," she said.

"Ma. Please. I have to get to America first before I can return."

She laughed. We hugged each other and she kissed me. I

turned away and left the house before she saw I was bit teary, too. I wanted her to feel only happiness for me.

———————◗◦◖———————

My father drove me to the ferry in Belfast that would take me to Liverpool. My mother had packed me two liverwurst sandwiches. I was too nervous to eat until I was safely aboard the freighter that would take me to New York.

My father and I did not find much of consequence to discuss on the hour-and-a-half trip to the capital city. He did, however, tell me a half-dozen times that his door would always be open to me. I suspected he thought there was a very small chance I'd be returning any time soon. But I chose instead to impute kinder motives to the old man. I knew I would miss him, too.

He hugged me on the pier before the final blast of the ship's whistle to board. Two tears escaped his eyes, making it hard to contain my own.

"We did pretty good, the two of us, all in all," he said. "Don't do anything I wouldn't do, son."

"That's exactly what I have in mind to do, Pop," I replied.

He laughed heartily, his chest heaving in and out, and chucked me on the shoulder. I was glad my last glimpse of my father was of him laughing. He remained on the pier until the ferry pulled from port and everything disappeared in the gathering mist.

I sat on one of the long benches, watching my fellow passengers huddle into their hoods and hats and scarves. There was not much else to look at. I shut my eyes and went over my grandma's Recipe for the Compression (or Expansion) of Time. I did not want to recite the wrong one. But I could not get either one to work.

An hour-and-a-half later, we pulled into Liverpool, also in the fog, though it was not as thick as on the open water. I took up my canvas satchel with leather handles, my apprentice's bag, and searched for Pier 12. The nimbuses and haloes around the lights in the port painted a mystical scene as though by an Old Master, a scene slightly faded by time and forgetting.

I found *HMS Argos*, a rust-bucket originally of Greek registration, and boarded as soon as I was allowed. Locating my cabin below deck, I set down my bag and sat down on the lumpy bunk. I'd built larger and better outfitted coffins for O'Riley.

The spare accommodations were the reason my passage was so cheap and why it took fourteen days, sailing to countless ports in the south of England and the west of Ireland before setting sail upon the Atlantic. My cabin was near one of the generators and I heard its unobtrusive hum. But when the engines started up, I thought the vibrations would rattle every bolt and rivet loose before we got underway.

My proximity to the engine room meant I spent more time up on deck, often in one of the hammocks the crew had set up and used.

If it was not too cold, at night I swayed gently in my cradle of stars. During the day, I sunned myself. Since I didn't have swim trunks for sunbathing, I wore just my Levi's. Some of the othe passengers thought I was a member of the crew.

Without changing scenery, and with no way to gauge speed or distance, I'd expected time would creep. But once we entered the wide ocean and bobbed among its waves and swells, time passed more quickly. I managed to go from anxiousness about leaving my homeland to nervousness about moving some place I'd never been before, and where I knew but a single person, my cousin Phaedre.

My heartbeat quickened the closer we got to New York. There was still no sign of Mr. Kattywampus who hadn't shown himself since I left Belfast. I forced myself to be optimistic and, as though on cue, he appeared up on deck that evening. He was announced when his silhouette blocked the brilliant sky awash with stars and a display of streaking meteors.

"Tomorrow, my boy, we shall set foot upon American soil. And there you shall celebrate your twenty-first anniversary on the earth."

He remained in the shadows. His pipe lit up his disembodied face.

"I shall tell you how to go about it, Fitzgerald."

"Go about what, Mr. Kattywampus?"

"Setting foot in a country that will be the land in which you will be buried. Always be respectful. It's important to do things right."

"All right," I said.

"Good, Fitzgerald McGuirk. Can you smell America?"

I stepped to the railing of the old freighter. Shutting my eyes and breathing in several lungs full of air, I detected on the night breeze a smell that was not salty. It was the smell of earth and humus, of plants and trees and dirt. I turned to tell the Old One at my shoulder, but he had vanished.

That night, my last upon the sea, I decided to occupy one of the hammocks. I was the only one on deck: just me and a sky full of stars, with the smell of American soil upon the wind.

Mr. Kattywampus visited my dream ere long and explained to me the Ritual Recipe for First Setting Foot in the New World. It seemed odd to me, but, then, everything he tells me seems at least as queer as I am.

Bayonne, New Jersey, rather than New York as I expected. It requires passage aboard another ferry to get me to the pier in Manhattan where, I hope, Phaedre awaits me. It is not a long trip.

I see her in the well-lighted waiting room through the dark window glass. It is two in the morning. She sleeps sprawled across two of the seats without armrests. I do not want to awaken her, but my shadow falls across her face. She jerks awake and springs to her feet.

"My God, Fitz, you're here," my cousin says, hugging me and spinning me around despite her small size. "Welcome to America, Fitz."

Phaedre's smile is brighter than the glaring fluorescent tubes overhead. We both seem a bit stunned that the other has grown up so much since last we laid eyes on one another.

"Wow. You're quite a woman now, Cuz," I tell her. "Quite a smashing woman at that."

"Thank you. And aren't you the hunk in your Levi's? Let's

have a look at you, Fitz."

"Hunk?" I ask.

"That's American for a good-looking, sexy bloke," she explains. "Why are you wearing only one boot, Fitz? What's that black stuff on your foot?"

"I didn't have time to wash my foot and get my sock and boot back on. The ferry was leaving."

"That explains nothing, Fitz, except how you got here. Try again."

"It's a custom in my family whenever we set foot in the New World for the first time."

"I have much the same family, Cuz. It sounds like a Kattywampus custom to me."

"I suppose it might be," I tell her, grinning. "Let me use the loo to wash my foot and get my boot back on.'

"That would be wise. We've got a long walk over to the Eight Avenue Express—the subway, the Tube. You can explain it to me on the way."

Nothing about America or New York City is within a hundred miles of how I pictured it. The lavatory is filthy. I support myself on the edge of the sink and put my muddy foot under the spigot. I slip on my sock and pull on my boot.

My cousin and I go through the smeary glass doors. The air smells equally of land and sea. It has been rain-freshened. The pavement glistens, though it is grimy beneath the film of water. I am amazed at the number of pedestrians and cars at such a late hour.

Unable to keep from looking up at the impossibly tall towers all agleam with lights and signs and beacons, I step off the curb prematurely, nearly getting flattened by a racing taxicab. I forgot about their driving on the wrong side of the road in America. Phaedre yanks me back in time.

I put my hands in the pockets of my leather jacket. Phaedre hooks her arm into the crook of my elbow. I feel like quite the studly hunk, as she puts it. She presses me for the explanation of the Ritual Recipe for First Setting Foot in the New World.

"Mr. Kattywampus suggested 'setting foot' someplace

could only be taken one way—literally. I had to place my naked foot in the first mud puddle I encountered in America. It had just rained and one of the service roads to the wharf was not paved."

"You are a unique and wonderful person, Fitz. I am proud to be your cousin. I hope for your sake your friend among the Old Ones is real."

"Of course he is real, Cuz. Is not my entire blesséd and magical life testament to the fact that I've had help? I have not forgotten my promise. I have asked him to let you see him."

We hear the subway train rumbling in its tube and rush down the many stairs to the platform. The air is stale and thick and heavy. The air in the train is better. I think it is air-conditioned. Even at half-past two in the morning, the subway car is packed. Phaedre takes the one available seat without trash on it.

At the last instant, Mr. Kattywampus gets on, the doors closing behind him. He rests his gnarled and wrinkled hand on the seat in front of Phaedre.

"There he is," I whisper, nodding my head down towards my unimaginary friend. I do not want to startle the other riders, unsure how they would react to an Old One aboard a New York City subway train. I wonder whether he paid his fare or simply appeared on this side of the turnstile.

Phaedre looks up at him, then at me, her eyes and mouth wide with astonishment.

"No one is a smelly old beggar, Phaedre," Mr. Kattywampus informs her. "We are all God's children."

He vanishes like someone at the corner of your eye, not even waiting for the next stop, which the squawking intercom on the A train tells us will be 59th Street—Columbus Circle.

"Oh my God, Fitz," my cousin says, her voice trembling and the blood draining from her face. "I didn't realize who he was at first. He really is real. I'm sorry for doubting you. The old fellow homed in on my thoughts and told me what I was thinking, word for word."

"He does that," I say. "I think it's an exercise to make sure you're listening to yourself."

"I don't know what to say, Fitz. I'm ashamed of myself. I

was so unkind."

"You're still my favorite cousin, Phaedre."

"I'm your only cousin on our fathers' side."

"And my only favorite among them," I tell her, winking.

She blows me a kiss. I notice that no one in New York notices anything, though I suspect they've taken in every scene. Each has told himself or herself their own story about who Phaedre and I and Mr. Kattywampus are to each other—if they saw him. I doubt any of their stories even grazes the truth.

The A train runs express to 125th Street in Harlem. We are at Phaedre's stop at 181st Street in no time. I cannot see the top of the escalator from the bottom we are so deep below ground.

We climb more stairs and ascend a steep hill on Fort Washington Avenue to her basement flat. Happily, my cousin does not even remove her coat before breaking out a bottle of Old Curmudgeon whisky and two glasses. I take off my biker jacket and tug off my boots.

"Sláinte," we toast one another.

"It looks like you might be a bit long for my davenport, Fitz."

"After my bunk aboard the freighter, the floor will be a prince's divan," I tell her.

I sit on the floor and she takes one of the two upholstered armchairs.

"Tomorrow we can work something else out," she says.

"Tomorrow maybe you can tell me how to go about getting my own flat."

"I've taken the day off work, Fitz. I'll get you acquainted with New York and then we can hang out at my favorite tavern down in The Bowery called *The Outer Burro.*

"The pub is around the corner from my little theater company, *Circus McGuirkus*, named after our family. I'm afraid there'll be a bit of work mixed in. I'm considering an actor for the lead in my next production. I'm pretty sure the part is his. I'd like you to meet him."

"Ah-hah," I say. "The matchmaker at work. Any idea which way he turns?"

"Probably anticlockwise like you, but I don't know for sure."

She pours more whisky in our glasses and at last takes off her coat.

"Starting on Monday, Fitz, you'll be designing and building the sets for *Circus McGuirkus*. There's another play coming up next month, plus a few other jobs I've lined up for you."

"Jeeze, thanks, Phaedre. Wow. My first position in New York."

"Your first *job* in New York," she corrects.

"Right," I say.

Her flat is warm and comfy. The boiler's steam pipes run overhead. Phaedre has cleverly disguised them with paint and bits of fabric to resemble the thick underground roots of an enormous tree. Her inventiveness has always been playful. The whisky—and my excitement, no doubt—have made me very tired. I lie back on Phaedre's thick shag carpet and shut my eyes for a moment.

———◦———

I awaken in the same position next morning, a blanket over me and a pillow beneath my head. I hear Phaedre stirring in the kitchen and sit up. I am still in my clothes. She brings me a mug of black coffee and Irish breakfast tea with milk for herself.

"How'd you sleep, Fitz?" she asks.

"Like a stone," I tell her, taking a sip of my head-clearing coffee. "It was so pleasant sleeping on something that didn't yaw and pitch and threaten to hurl me to the floor."

"You're already on the floor, Fitz," Phaedre says, smiling. "Do you want to shower? Do you have clean clothes?"

"In my bag," I say.

"Good," she replies. "We won't have to do laundry. That puts us ahead. We can get breakfast at the café on the corner. Oh, by the way, happy birthday."

I nod and clink her teacup with my coffee mug. I finish my coffee and take clean underwear into the bathroom. The water is wonderfully hot and the room steams up. I feel as though I am aboard the *Argos* again. In the fog, Mr. Kattywampus speaks, whether back on the ship or here in Phaedre's shower, I'm not certain.

"Congratulations, my boy, on attaining your twenty-first anniversary on the earth. I am prepared to grant the fulfillment of one wish before day's end, whatever you please—within reason, of course. Be circumspect in what you choose, Fitzgerald McGuirk. It is not your happiness alone that depends on it."

"Thank you, Mr. Kattywampus. I appreciate that you aren't putting any pressure on me."

"You're welcome, my boy," he says, laughing, his smile illuminating the shower steam. "The cost will only be the shirt off your back: not a high price at all, considering."

"Considering what?" I ask, but he has vanished like mist on the breeze.

———————◦○◦———————

My cousin has become much more competitive and take-charge since she left the Old Sod five years ago. She does everything at a New York pace. I wouldn't have minded lying in this morning. Phaedre's carpet is very comfortable.

She produced a list of apartments to check out in The Bronx, the only neighborhood she thinks I can afford. I wound up signing the lease and paying the deposit on the second flat we looked at. It was a formerly elegant six-storey building facing a wide street called, not surprisingly, "Broadway." It is the same Broadway of flashing lights and crowds of theatre-goers, except that, up in The Bronx, elevated tracks run down the middle of it. My building is six blocks beyond the last stop on the 1 train. There are soccer pitches and equestrian stables and tennis courts in the nearby park.

Phaedre told me my next steps ought to be acquiring carpentry tools, a few sticks of furniture, and maybe some dressier clothes in case I "happen to meet someone." I found acceptable furniture—a bed, table, chairs, a dresser, and two lamps—at a second-hand shop. I bought new hand tools—saw, hammer, level, chalk-line, spanners, etc.—from the ironmongers, the hardware store, ready to give them my own marks of use and wear.

I resisted the idea, as did American writer Henry David Thoreau, of any new enterprise that required new clothes. Phaedre, marking my birthday, insisted on buying me a new jumper—what Americans call a *sweater* —and a pair of black Levi's, since I refused to wear any other pants or brand of jeans.

The furniture, tools, and new clothes will all be delivered to my apartment in care of the building superintendent, a fellow Mick hailing from County Armagh. As Phaedre urged, I handed the super a generous tip.

The day's errands and purchases completed, we headed downtown to *The Outer Burro*, nearly at the opposite end of New York City. We'd just managed to duck inside when thunder and lightning rumbled and flashed overhead, and a downpour descended. I added that to my day's good fortune, wondering what part, if any, Mr. Kattywampus had played in our staying dry.

"Lloyd," Phaedre tells the barkeep, "this is my cousin Fitzgerald McGuirk, just one day in America."

"Pleased to meet you, young man," he says, extending his hand to me.

"It's also his birthday today, Lloyd, his twenty-first, in fact."

"Congratulations, Fitzgerald. On the house," he adds, setting a bottle of Old Curmudgeon whisky and two glasses before Phaedre and me.

"Thank you, Lloyd," my cousin and I say.

"To a most successful day," she tells me, raising her glass. "How do you feel, Fitz?"

"A bit breathless," I reply. "It's all happening sort of fast. And the day's not over."

"This is New York City, Fitz. If you stand still, you'll be run over. Happy Birthday."

Phaedre pours more whisky in my glass though I hadn't finished the previous one. Mr. Kattywampus stands at my right hand, in front of the last barstool. He has difficulty climbing up without a little boost from magic. I order a glass for him, but Lloyd does not know here to set it. He does not appear to see my friend. I pour some Old Curmudgeon in the Old One's glass. Lloyd watches me from the corner of his eye.

"Sláinte," Mr. Kattywampus says.

"Sláinte," I reply.

Phaedre turns to me.

"I see your little friend has joined your birthday celebration," she says, nodding to him.

"He asks that you not call him little, Phaedre. He can be any size he wishes but chooses to be compact for economy's sake."

"I see. Say *Hello* from me."

Apparently my cousin can see Mr. Kattywampus but cannot hear him.

Mr. Kattywampus asks me whether I have readied my birthday wish. I tell him I have but prefer to convey it wordlessly. Saying a wish out loud might jinx it.

"I understand," he says, closing his eyes.

"That's an excellent wish, Fitzgerald McGuirk," he says, after reading my mind. "I am proud of you."

As my mentor raises his glass, there is another loud clap of thunder. The front door bursts open and a blast of cool air rushes in. A young man, soaked to the skin, walks in, squelching up to the bar.

He is the brown-skinned man I first beheld in my dream years ago. Everything about him glistens: his dark skin, his black hair and T-shirt, and his wet Levi's.

"Antonio Morales?" my cousin asks.

"Yes," he replies. "Sorry to be late. Ran into some heavy weather."

I cannot take my eyes off him. I know I am staring, but he's bound me in a spell. Phaedre introduces him to me, but my heart pounds too loudly to hear what he says. My mouth seems disconnected from my brain. Nothing comes out.

Lloyd hands Antonio a couple of white bar towels that his wet Levi's stain blue in a pattern that looks like tie-dye. He laughs, his smile making me forget the clever quip I was about to utter.

Mr. Kattywampus jumps down from his stool and urges

me to take his place. Antonio sits between me and Phaedre. I can feel his heat through his wet clothes. My heart pounds.

Antonio shakes my hand and orders a Mexican beer.

"My cousin Fitz is the one who gave me the idea for the production we'll be doing, Antonio. You have him to thank."

"Me?" I ask. "What play are you putting on?"

"*The Wilde One*," Phaedre says, "with an E. The members of both motorcycle gangs are queer, giving things a bit of a twist. Written by playwright Doric Wilson. It's quite droll."

"*Jimmy, maybe better put some more beer on ice,*" Antonio says, quoting the line from the movie.

We all laugh. If he's trying to impress Phaedre, I think he hit his mark. His arrow shot me, too.

I see Antonio is shivering, a combination of his wet clothes and the air conditioning and his cold beer. Standing up, I offer him my leather jacket. At last I have struck him speechless.

Antonio tries to reject my offer, but at last relents. I hold my jacket out for him to slip his arms into. We're pretty much the same size. It gives me a thrill to see him wearing it.

Mr. Kattywampus waves good-night. I remember his saying my wish would cost me the shirt off my back. I smile at him.

"Strange little guy," Antonio says. "I see him on the subway sometimes."

"I'm astonished. You saw him, too, Antonio?" Phaedre asks.

"Yeah, he's not *that* short," Antonio replies, making everyone laugh again.

He orders another Dos Equis and Phaedre pours a tad more whisky in our glasses.

"Fitz signed a lease today on an apartment up in The Bronx. Didn't you say that's where you live, Antonio?"

"Yeah, but The Bronx is a big place. Where abouts, Fitz?"

"Right on Broadway."

"What's the cross street?

I look to Phaedre.

"252nd Street," she tells him. "His flat overlooks Van Cortlandt Park."

"I'm not far from there, four blocks, at 248th."

"Then why don't you keep my jacket for tonight, Antonio. You're all wet. I'll be fine. Tomorrow and Sunday I'll be moving more stuff into my apartment. How about coming by for supper on Sunday? I mean, if you're free. You can return my jacket then."

"Yeah, I'm free. But I'd like to bring our supper. You've both been very kind. Will you be there, too, Phaedre?"

My cousin looks to me for the answer.

"Yes," I tell him. "Of course Phaedre's coming. Won't we be a jolly bunch?"

"Are you both OK with Mexican? My *chile rellenos* are not The Mild Ones."

Phaedre and I nod, smiling at his word play. Finishing our drinks, we say good-night to Lloyd. I leave him a generous gratuity for his hospitality.

It is a bit of a walk to the Underground at Chambers Street, but I enjoy the chance to admire Antonio as he walks between my cousin and me in my leather jacket. He tells us about growing up in New Mexico, a real cowboy. He enacts one of the rumble scenes from *The Wild One* as we walk down the sidewalk. He takes on several parts in quick succession, causing heads to turn. We laugh. I can't wait to see him in *The Wilde One*.

The three of us take the 1 train uptown, though that is less convenient for Phaedre and me. I don't mind keeping Antonio in sight as long as I can. It is too noisy to carry on much of a conversation in the subway without shouting. He touches my hand and winks, giving me a heart-thumping thrill.

My cousin and I leave Antonio at 181st Street as he continues on the 1 train up to The Bronx. It's a bit of a hike from St. Nicholas Avenue over to Phaedre's flat on Ft. Washington Avenue.

"Not bad for a day's work, Fitz," Phaedre tells me, as we walk. "But I'm afraid I'll have to disappoint you, Cuz. I can't possibly come to supper on Sunday. I don't want to say something that might interfere in the Old One's magic, if that's what is going on. I can come another time."

I fold my arms around her. We are surrounded by New Yorkers who don't notice us.

"Thank you, Phaedre. Were you expecting Antonio and me to hit it off?"

"No, not expecting. Just hoping you would. Happy Birthday, Fitz."

"I don't know whether Mr. Kattywampus had Antonio put the glamour on me or not. I've never felt quite like this before, Cuz. Never. I've been gob-smacked and smitten."

"Sounds like plain old love at first sight to me, Fitz, though I wouldn't be surprised if perhaps there were a wee bit of magic woven in."

"If this is my first day in the New World, I can't imagine what the future holds," I say.

Phaedre smiles, and takes hold of my arm as we trudge uphill to her basement flat.

MY TWO PAPAS

I hear a Harley rumble down the road and park out front. My father must be home from work early and I scramble to collect my flash cards before he sees them. He does not approve of my learning magic, much less practicing what I have learned. I stuff the colorful cards and my magic book under the sofa cushions and make busy washing dishes at the kitchen sink.

When my papa doesn't park his bike in the back yard for the night, it means he will be going out again after supper, likely to The Ornery Burro, and coming home late. There is nothing for supper in the refrigerator. I hope he has remembered to bring something, maybe a flank steak and a couple of peppers to make *fajitas*. I'm hungry thinking about it. I check to see that we have tortillas and corn and onions.

The loud knocking at the front door startles me. Did he forget his keys? Why didn't he go around back? The kitchen door is always unlocked. The rapping on the screen door continues and I swing open the inside door.

It is another motorcycle rider, covered head to foot in dust, his helmet in the crook of his arm. It has hardly rained all month, otherwise he'd be splattered with mud. I see over his shoulder that he also rides a Harley-Davidson, but unlike my papa's black Ironhead Sportster, it is a fancy blue-and-white Electra. I'm not even looking at the guy standing on the porch and would never be able to pick him out in a line-up. His Harley has orange-and-black New York license tags.

"Excuse me, son," the man says. His accent sounds British. He slaps his leather jacket and Levi's as though that's going to get him undusted. I do not unlatch the screen door.

He has wavy dark hair and piercing blue eyes. He's sun-tanned, but is clearly an Anglo, almost the opposite of my father and me. The guy looks a little bit familiar. Maybe my father brought him home once.

"I'm looking for Antonio Morales," he says. "I got directions at the gas station, but maybe I took a wrong turn."

"Yeah, maybe you did," I tell him, folding my arms across my chest.

"Do you know where Mr. Morales lives, young man?"

"Yeah, I do."

I decide to let him squirm. He shifts his weight onto his other foot.

"Would you mind giving me directions? My name's Fitzgerald McGuirk. Call me Fitz. I'm a friend of Mr. Morales."

"Oh, brother," I say. "Where'd he meet you? The Ornery Burro?"

"Where? No, I hooked up with Antonio when he visited New York City on his vacation a couple months back. Do you know where he lives?"

"Yeah, I do."

"I'm sorry you're in a bad mood, kid, but the sooner you tell me, the sooner I'll be on my way."

"He lives here," I announce, "but he's at work."

"Mind if I come in to wait for him?"

"Yeah, I do. My father doesn't like me letting strangers in the house."

I say nothing more, hoping the guy goes away.

"OK. I get it, kiddo. Vampires and devils can only get in if you invite them. And you don't ever want to grant them power over you by revealing your name to them. Only one thing wrong with that."

"What's that?" I ask.

"I'm just an ordinary man—well, almost ordinary. Like you, I know a little magic, that's all."

"How do you know what I can do, mister?"

"The name's Fitz, remember? It takes one to know one. My grandma began showing me things when I was about ten years old. It helps to have a teacher, José."

I draw closer to the screen door to get a better look at him. I think his smile could easily bewitch someone. *Did he bewitch my papa?*

"No, I didn't bewitch anyone. I'll wait for Antonio out here on the porch then, if I may."

"OK by me. Suit yourself."

I head back to the kitchen, but turn to have another look at the guy. He knew what I was thinking. I don't remember telling him my name, either.

Fitz sets his helmet over the finial of the handrail and plunks himself down in one of the rockers. He puts his feet, in their dusty boots, on the porch railing, just like my papa does. My legs don't quite reach yet.

I don't care for any of the guys my father brings home. Maybe this one is different. At least Fitz and my father share an interest in motorcycles. That's more than he has in common with most of the losers he meets. My papa did talk favorably about someone he met in New York on his trip, but I don't remember the guy's name. Maybe this is him.

After a short while, Fitz gets up out of the rocker. I think he's leaving, but his helmet is still on the finial. He retrieves a canteen from one of his saddle bags and returns to the front porch. He takes off his leather jacket and hangs it over the back of the rocker before resuming his place in it. After another little while, he asks whether he can use the bathroom or whether he should just water the chamisa in the front yard. I tell him the outhouse is out back.

I watch him from the kitchen window. He's about my father's size, lean and muscular. He's courteous enough to latch the outhouse door when he's finished. It keeps critters out. I decide maybe Fitz is all right, and feel bad for being so unfriendly. My papa emphasizes to me the importance of kindness. I have not been kind to his friend—if he really is Papa's friend.

Though I know it's not going to happen, I still wish my father would fall for a beautiful and intelligent woman. If he did it once with my mother, why couldn't he do it again? The magic I've been trying on him hasn't been working. He still likes men. I guess I wouldn't exactly be in favor of a baby brother or sister running around the house anyhow. Maybe it's OK the way it is.

I unlatch the front screen door and lean my head out. Fitz has his eyes closed and must not have heard the squealing hinges. I was going to ask him if he wanted a glass of cold water from our refrigerator. It looks like he could use some water on the outside, too. Maybe he'll want to wash up before my father gets home.

He jerks awake and plants his boots on the porch floor.

"I sure wouldn't mind washing up a little if you'll tell me where," he says, as though he'd been reading my mind again. "A garden hose'd be fine, son," he adds.

I don't like his calling me "son." One father is enough. I'm not letting him in the house.

"There's a pump out back by the horse trough," I tell him. "I'll fetch you a towel and washcloth and some soap."

Fitz thanks me and goes to the back yard. I watch him strip off his jean jacket and black T-shirt. He works the pump, splashing his face and chest with the ice cold water without flinching. Then he soaps up, even his hair, and rinses himself with the chipped enamel pot we keep by the trough for that purpose. He dries himself with the towel.

Rinsing his T-shirt in the trough, he wrings it out and hangs it and the towel over the old hitching post. He sits down in the sun on the cottonwood stump beside the barn.

I finish washing the dishes from breakfast just as I hear my father's roar and see the cloud of dust follow him into the back yard. I greet him at the back door with a hug and a bottle of Dos Equis beer. He has not forgotten the groceries for our supper. I take the paper sack from him.

"Who the hell's Harley is that parked out front, José?"

Before I can answer, Papa's friend rounds the corner of the barn and walks to the back porch.

"You're the last person I expected to see, Fitz," my father

says, extending his hand, then hugging him. "I'm happy to see you. I didn't think you'd get here for another couple of days. Bring another beer, son."

"You have the last one, Papa."

"There's more beer in my other saddle bag. I'll take one of the warm ones. Here, Fitz. Take the cold beer."

"I'm Irish. We don't care for our beer too cold, remember?"

"That's right. OK. I can't believe you rode all the way out here, buddy. How far is it?"

"About two thousand miles, give or take."

"Jesús y Maria," my father exclaims.

"And let's not forget about José," Fitz says, turning to me and smiling.

I am happy I got a chance to be kind to him before Papa got home. My father and his friend sit beneath the shade of the deep eaves on the bench made from a split log. They stretch their legs out. I fetch the beer from my father's saddle bag. I open one for Fitz and hand it to him.

"Thank you, José," he says

"Can we handle a supper guest?" my father asks.

"I think so, Papa."

He smiles at me. I wish he'd use his smile more often.

"Do you want some help with supper, José?" Fitz asks.

"I can take care of it," I tell him. "Thanks for asking. I've got Kitchen Patrol for supper during the week 'cause I get home first. Papa's got weekend meals. That's our arrangement."

Taking the groceries into the kitchen, I unpack the bag. I open the kitchen window slowly and quietly. I don't want to miss what my father and his friend are saying to each other out back. Their conversation isn't very interesting, mostly about their bikes and Fitz's long trip out here to New Mexico from New York. I have homework to do.

Remembering my book of magic and the incantation flash cards I hid beneath the sofa cushions, I take them up to my room. I smile, thinking how I got Margaret from school to like me after I prepared one of my magic recipes for her.

I'm not sure it will work on two guys, though. I'd just like my papa to find someone who makes him happy.

———————◦———————

After supper, my father and Fitz open another two beers and sit out back again, conversing beneath the stars. I go up to my room, claiming I need to study some more.

Though I have my window open wide, I can make out only the occasional word. Laughter drowns out most of their conversation.

I practice my flash cards once more before turning in, hoping to help my father and his friend get along. I like Fitz better than anyone my father has brought home and hope he is good for Papa. Lighting sagebrush incense, I waft the smoke with the eagle's feather that floated down to me on my last birthday.

I fall asleep like a stone plunging into a deep pond, dreaming of Papa and Fitz riding the Appaloosa horses we used to have when I was a little boy. I do not remember their names. I recall only that my papa and I were very sad when the man who bought them came to take them away in his trailer. It was the only time I saw my papa cry.

———————◦———————

I come downstairs the next morning to make coffee for my father and Fitz, and to pack my lunch for school. I find them already drinking coffee, sitting at the kitchen table in their long-johns and T-shirts.

"Sorry. Did we wake you?" my father asks.

"No," I say, yawning. "Good morning," I tell my papa's friend.

"Good morning, José," he replies, flashing his smile.

I refill their cups and ask to be excused. Going up to my room, I get dressed. I put on a sweatshirt first, but change into the green plaid flannel shirt Margaret told me looked good on me. When I think of her, she is always smiling.

Though I try to make sense of the words floating up from downstairs, my father's and Fitz's talking is just beyond earshot.

When I return to the kitchen, they are dressed. Fitz's Levi's look much cleaner than yesterday. I realize he has hung his dirty jeans over our horseless hitching post in the back yard.

My father stands at the stove cooking our breakfast: three burritos with eggs, green chile, and spicy sausage. It's been a while since Papa cooked breakfast during the week. We usually have toast or cereal with fruit.

"You're going to make quite a catch some day, Papa," I tell him, using the phrase on him that he likes to tease me with.

He looks at me sternly, as if I'm about to receive a reprimand, but he winds up smiling at me. Fitz chuckles.

My father serves us. He makes excellent burritos, with cheddar cheese from the old woman with the goats.

I gobble up my breakfast with a glass of milk. When we are finished, I gather up the plates and set them in the sink, pumping water until it is full.

My father puts his hand on Fitz's shoulder and bends to kiss him on the cheek.

"If you're going to hang around a few more days, Fitz, I'll bring home some extra chow."

"I thought I might," Fitz says. "All right with you, José?" he asks.

"Me? Sure. Why not?" I reply. "Why does it matter what I think?"

"We'll talk about it tonight, all right?" Papa says.

I hand my father the shopping list I'd drawn up. He folds it, stuffing it into the pocket of his denim workshirt. Fitz gives him some money. Papa takes the keys for the old turquoise pickup from the hook and heads out the door. We are a bit behind time.

"See you tonight," he says to Fitz, who stands at the back screen door.

I chase after my father and climb into the pickup he'd sanded by hand and painted with a brush. I wave to Fitz.

I hope Fitz stays for at least a few more days—maybe longer. I want to know what kind of magic he can do. My magic book isn't enough. I need a teacher.

My papa drops me off just up the road where the school bus picks me up and continues on his way to Mila-Grow Nursery

& Greenhouse where he is their landscaper.

I sit at the back of the bus, ignoring my friends. I've got a lot to think about and don't feel like talking. If Margaret took my bus, though, instead of the South Side bus where she lives, I'd definitely talk to her. She's the most interesting girl in my class.

School was about usual that day. I don't recall any of it except for Margaret remarking how well my green shirt complemented my dark complexion. I wonder if she could tell when I blushed.

When I get home from school, Papa's friend straddles the peak of the barn roof, shirtless in just his dirty pair of Levi's and a faded Harley-Davidson cap he wears backwards. The barn sits beneath the dappled sunlight filtering through the arc of tall cottonwoods surrounding it.

"Down in a minute, José. Just finishing up."

I like that my papa's friend doesn't waste a lot of words. After putting my book-bag on the kitchen table, I take a long swallow from the pitcher of cold water in the icebox. Standing at the screen door, I holler up to Fitz.

"Would you like a cold beer?" I ask him.

"Sure," he replies. "By the time I get down, it'll be just the right temperature."

Fitz hammers in another cedar shingle. I go back inside and open a bottle of beer which I put on the little table beneath the eaves out back. Then I take my books up to my room and change into my after-school clothes: old jeans and a T-shirt. My breath catching, I watch Fitz from my window as he climbs down our rickety ladder from the peak of the barn loft.

I go downstairs and take a Coke from the fridge, meeting Fitz outside. He fills his cap with water from the trough and splashes it over himself, drying himself with his T-shirt and tugging it on. He smells anyway. Sitting down in the other wood chair, he clinks my bottle of Coke and takes a sip of his Dos Equis.

"Sláinte," he says. "That's Irish for 'To your health.'"

"My papa and I say 'Salud,'" I tell him.

"Salud," he repeats.

"So you met my papa on his vacation to New York?" I ask. "And then you ride like two thousand miles? Sounds kinda serious for such a short time. Is there something going on between you and my father?"

Fitz turns on his movie star smile.

"If there is anything going on, José, it's got a long, slow fuse. Your father and I have known each other since high school, when we were your age."

"What?" I say. "I thought you two just met this past summer."

I lean forward in my chair. My mouth is dry and I take a sip of Coke. It is too sweet.

"Not hardly. Antonio and I have known each other for more than fifteen years. Before his visit this summer, though, we hadn't seen each other in ten years. We kinda fell out of touch."

"Yeah, I'd say," I remark.

"Do you recall my last visit out here to Red Willow, José? Your papa had just inherited this house from his grandma. You would've been only about five."

"I'm not sure I remember. Give me a minute," I say, closing my eyes.

I picture Fitz's face leaning down to me, smiling. He hoists me to his shoulders so I can pick apples from our orchard for Hallowe'en. Papa holds a basket.

I open my eyes.

"I do remember you," I tell him. "So did my papa sleep with you when he was in New York?"

"He did, but you know, José, I'd be more comfortable talking about that after your papa gets home. Why don't you tell me how you learned to read a person's mind?"

I smile and feel my face get hot. I wonder if I'm blushing.

"Yeah, you're blushing, kiddo, though you've got to be looking for it," Fitz tells me. "It's also good to know how to close the door of your mind to anyone you don't want reading you. Can you do that, José?"

"No," I admit. "Maybe you could teach me some time."

"Sure. I haven't had anyone to share magic with since my grandma died. Closing the door to your thoughts is important, José. It's also one of the easiest ways of becoming invisible."

"Really? Invisible? Holy shit."

"I don't think you realize how much hard work and concentration and practice it takes to become see-through for even a minute. It takes a lot of discipline."

"Why is everything so hard?" I ask. "I can't wait to learn magic so I won't have to work."

"Before you throw your retirement party, José, you might want to finish high school. It comes in handy for all sorts of things. There's a lot of math involved in magic."

"It figures. There's math in everything."

"Sure there is. But if you do well in school, you'll do well in magic. We'll ask your papa if it's all right for me to teach you certain things. How often do you practice the lessons in your magic book and flash cards?"

I realize my thoughts must have leaked out.

"I know about your book of magic, José. I'm the one who left it with your father when I couldn't be here to teach you."

"I practice almost every day, Fitz. But a lot of it doesn't make sense to me. I'm not always sure what I'm doing."

"It wasn't always clear to me at first, either. My grandma helped me. Now I'm here to help you," he says, ruffling my hair. "That's one of my reasons for being here."

"And what's another?" I ask him, taking a swallow of my cola.

"To see whether your father and I can get along well enough to live under the same roof. I'm hoping we can. How would you feel about that, son?"

His question startles me. I don't know what to tell him. Things are moving awfully fast. I like Fitz, but I'm not sure how crazy I am about his staying with us full-time. My father and I are kind of settled into our routine.

"Fair enough," he tells me. "We'll take everything real slow, all right?"

Fitz has finished his beer and I my cola. I go into the kitchen to fetch another beer for him and a glass of cold water for my-self. My papa drives up in the pickup. I open a bottle of beer for him, too.

Papa takes two sacks of groceries from the back of the pickup. There is also a thick wooden beam and a pile of lumber and cedar shingles lying in the bed. Fitz takes one of the grocery bags and follows him into the house. I hand them their bottles of beer: one warm, the other cold.

My papa tousles my hair. He and Fitz hug each other and give each other a peck. I'm surprised they don't stick together they are both so sweaty and smelly from their day's work.

I unpack the grocery sacks and put things away.

"What should I make for supper, Papa?"

"It's on the front seat of the truck, José. I thought you de-served a break."

I rush outside. There's a large plastic sack from Taco Take-Out in the pickup, still warm and filling the cab with aromas that make me instantly hungry. I think the tacos my papa and I make taste better, but the take-out ones are a lot less work.

I set the table and Papa distributes our supper. There's a tub of tomato and green onion salad and a cardboard box of sopapillas for dessert. I set the jar of honey on the table and we sit down. Papa asks Fitz to say our grace.

"Great Spirit, thank you for bringing me home again to Red Willow. Thank you for the food you set before us and for the fellowship we at this table share."

I had not expected such a good prayer from Fitz.

"Why not?" Fitz asks me, talking through the first bite of his taco.

"Manners," my father reminds his friend. "Are you two talking through the airwaves?"

"We are," Fitz tells him. "José thought I said a good grace."

"That was nice of you, José. I hope you and Fitz can get along," my papa says, turning to each of us and smiling, taco sauce dripping down to his chin. He wipes his mouth with several of the thin paper napkins from Taco Take-Out. Fitz finishes his second taco and starts in on his salad.

"So. Did Fitz teach you any new tricks today?" my father asks.

"Wait. I thought you didn't like me practicing magic."

"I didn't want you trying it on your own, José. You could get hurt—or hurt someone else. Fitz is here to help you learn how to do it right. He's had a lot more practice."

"Is he going to live with us?" I ask. "Why can't I just have a normal family, you know, a man and a woman. Why is this happening to me?"

My papa swallows hard and glares at me.

"This isn't only happening to you, José. Don't be so selfish. Fitz and I have had to deal with being queer our whole lives. It's been no picnic, son."

"Your papa and I didn't just decide to like men, José," Fitz tells me. "This is how God made us. Did you decide to like Margaret instead of one of the boys in your class?"

"You know about Margaret?" I say, startled that Papa's friend knows this.

"I suggested you might want to learn how to close the door to your thoughts, José. For what it's worth, I think you would've won Margaret's heart without magic."

"You're spying on me," I tell him.

"No, I'm not, José. It's actually hard to tune you out. Your door is always open and you're kind of a loudmouth."

My father laughs. He finishes his supper and passes each of us one of the puffy pasties from the cardboard box. We drip honey over our *sopapillas*.

"We'll continue our discussion later, José," my father tells me. "Fitz and I are going to take our baths out back in the trough There are no dishes, so just get down to your homework."

"Yes, Papa."

Fitz tugs off his biker boots and my papa removes his workboots. I hand them each a towel and washcloth from the bathroom, a curtained enclosure in the corner of the kitchen where we take our baths in winter with hot water from the wood stove. My father and Fitz go out back. They hang a blanket over the wash line for privacy.

I go up to my room. It's stuffy, so I open my window. I try to write the essay for my homework assignment: *What Is a Family?*

There is so much laughter and splashing from outside that it's hard to concentrate. It is quiet for a while and then the shifting wind brings their voices upstairs. I set down my pen.

"So. Do we spill the rest of the *frijoles* to José?" my father asks his friend.

"Look, Antonio, if we're gonna make a go of this, we can't keep things from José. It's time. He deserves to know everything. He's old enough. He's a smart kid."

"I'm still not sure how it even happened, buddy. Hypatia knew we both liked boys more than girls," my father says, referring to my mother.

"I don't think we quite knew we liked boys yet ourselves," Fitz remarks.

I think maybe I shouldn't be listening in, but I can't help it. Their voices are carried on the wind. I hear one of them working the pump handle to refill the trough. They yowl about the ice-cold water.

"I think Hypatia just wanted to see you and me make out, Fitz, that's all. It was pretty innocent. Things only got out of hand when we started in on that bottle of tequila you brought over to her house."

My papa's friend laughs.

"Next thing I knew," Fitz says, "we were all naked on the carpet among the sofa cushions and pillows and our pile of clothes, Hypatia between you and me."

"Well, at least you and I got to say we'd finally done it with a girl."

"First and last time," Fitz remarks.

I hear water gurgling in the sluice out to the garden. They are draining the old horse trough. The screen door slams. There is clattering in the kitchen.

I decide to wait a few minutes before going downstairs. My father and Fitz, sitting at the kitchen table, are in fresh longjohns and clean shirts.

"Would you care for a beer, José? Just a little."

"Sure, Papa."

"It's such a fine evening," Fitz says. "Why don't we sit out back?"

We take up our glasses and Papa brings the bottle of tequila from the cupboard. I know something important is about to happen. My father hardly ever lets me drink beer and he never drinks tequila except on special occasions.

We sit at the little table beneath the eaves. He and Fitz park themselves on the log bench. I pull up a chair. I see their rinsed-out Levi's hanging over the hitching post.

My papa snaps the cap off the bottle of beer and fills my short glass almost to the top. He pours the rest, half-and-half, into his and Fitz's glasses.

My papa places his hand on his friend's thigh as though it were an armrest. He was never so relaxed in front of me with any of the other chums he brought home.

We clink our three glasses together. I take a sip of beer.

"So what do you want to know, José?" my father asks. "We promise to tell you the truth. You are old enough."

"Why don't we start with why Mama left?" I say.

"Your mama wanted to have you, José. You know that. She loved you very much. But she didn't think she could raise you. She wanted to go to college and study astronomy. She wanted to do what was best for all of us. That includes your Uncle Fitz."

"I don't understand," I tell my father.

My papa looks to his friend.

"After your mother had you, José," Uncle Fitz says, "she moved East to attend college on her scholarship. Remember, all of us were only seventeen at the time. Times were different then, in 1960. I was going to move in with your papa and help raise you, but neither your papa nor I was ready to raise a young son together. We fought all the time. So I wound up moving to New York—like your mother. My cousin Phaedre found me a job as a carpenter building theater sets."

"Did you see my mama when you both lived in New York, Uncle Fitz?"

"Not often, José. We traveled in very different circles. Your mama went among her educated friends at Columbia University. I was a queer carpenter hanging out in The Bronx."

"So, *Tio*," I say to him. "That means *Uncle*. Why did you come out here again, *Tio*?"

"Mostly to help you with your magic, José. And to see if your papa and I have learned anything in the last ten years about living together."

I sip my beer to make it last. When my father and Fitz finish their beer, my father pours a little tequila in each of their glasses. The two friends look back and forth at each other, then over at me.

"I'd like Fitz to stay, son—to live with us. An extra pair of hands would come in handy around here—to say nothing of a second paycheck."

"Is that all there is to it, Papa? A little extra money? I could get a job after school."

My father smiles.

"No, José. That's not all of it. I love Fitz—an awful lot. I'm hoping we can stay together. We'd like to give it a try, anyway—if you agree."

My papa leans towards his friend and kisses him. It is the first time I have seen Papa kiss another man on the mouth. It doesn't look as strange—as queer—as I thought it would. Love is love, I guess.

"You're right, José," Fitz tells me. "Love is love, and I love your father a whole lot, too."

My father pours a little more tequila in their glasses. They clink them together.

"Can I please have more beer?" I ask, waiting to see which of them will answer *Yes*.

Instead, they both utter emphatic *Nos* at the same instant.

Uncle Fitz is not going to be the pushover I'd hoped for when my papa tells me I can't do something. Still, Papa's friend is pretty easy to like. He doesn't talk down to me and he's honest with me, telling me what he really thinks. I don't love him yet, but maybe in a while.

"So then which of you is really my father?" I ask, looking from one to the other.

"We're not really sure, José," my father says. "We both made love to your mama that same night. We all got a little bit drunk."

"Just a little bit drunk?" I ask.

Fitz smiles. "No, we got a lot drunk, José," he admits. "Your father and I found ourselves on top of each other, first him and then me, rubbing our privates together and getting excited."

"Then your mama got between us," my father says, continuing their story. "She guided first me and then your Uncle Fitz inside her until we came, probably not more than three minutes apart. We were all virgins before that night.

"So, in answer to your question, José, we never figured it out. You look more like me, but you've got your uncle's special talents. Does it matter? Can't we both be your father?"

"I don't know," I reply. "That's not quite how I learned it in biology class. It's usually one sperm and one egg, you know?"

"I'm not always sure how magic works or if magic was even involved," Uncle Fitz tells me. "You really could be both of ours, José. Love is a special form of magic whose math is really quite simple but whose geometry is impossibly complicated.

"Please promise your father and me that you won't repeat our mistakes by having premarital sex with Margaret. It forces you to make choices you are too young to make."

"Don't worry, Tio. It wouldn't be *premarital* sex."

"No? Why not, José?"

"Because Margaret and I are not planning on getting married."

It takes Tio and Papa a few seconds to realize I'm joking. They laugh though they try not to.

"Very funny," my papa says. "Consequences aren't always what you expect, son. Here we are, dealing with the outcome of a dalliance from fifteen years ago. It hasn't been easy, but I am glad it brought you into the world, José. And I'm happy my best friend has come home."

The waxing crescent moon is rising over The Mountain.

The sky is studded with stars. We all stand up. I step to the end of the porch. My father and Uncle Fitz look at me.

I draw a streak across the sky above the corral with my finger. "Look," I say.

A few seconds later, a meteor follows the path I have traced upon the indigo heavens. I'm not making it happen. I just know where the meteors are going to go. Three more follow which I also draw on the sky

"You get that from your mother," my father tells me, "with all her interest in astronomy. You've certainly got your mother's brains—when you choose to use them."

"That's a pretty neat trick, José," Tio tells me. "Maybe you can show me some time."

"Maybe," I say, grinning. "I'll trade you for a lesson on closing the door of my mind."

"Deal," Uncle Fitz says, shaking my hand. "You are an exceptional young man, José," he tells me, smiling his high-beam smile.

"Yes, I am exceptional, Tio," I reply. "Just like my mama, and like you and Papa—my two papas."

My father puts the cork in the bottle of tequila. Fitz stretches and yawns. We go into the kitchen. I rinse our glasses and put them on the drainboard. My head feels a little strange, sort of wobbly.

"I'm going to cook supper tomorrow, José. Leave it to me," my papa says. "After school you can give your Tio a hand fixing the barn door, OK?"

"Sure," I tell him. "I like building stuff a lot more than I like cooking."

"It's good to know both," Tio tells me.

Papa and Tio hug me good-night. My father puts his hand on Fitz's shoulder and they walk to the bedroom. I switch off the kitchen light and go up to my room.

After lighting a stick of sagebrush, I get undressed and climb beneath just the sheet in my shorts. It's a mild evening.

My head swirls, less from my short glass of beer than from all the twists and turns of my parents' story, whether two or three of them, I'm still not sure. It confirms my suspicion that grown-ups screw up and misbehave way more than they're comfortable admitting, especially to someone like me who's in the early stages of learning how to screw up.

I can see Papa and Tio are good to one another. Each deserves some happiness in his life. I hope it works out for them—for all of us. That is my prayer tonight.

———————●○●———————

The moon rises up to my window. I realize I am dreaming. Clouds drift across the moon.

No, it is not the moon. It is my mother's face. She wears a veil that flutters around her.

Behind her is the round window at church, peering like the moon over her shoulder.

I look down at my hands. They hold a white satin pillow. There is a ring on the pillow.

The ring frames a circle like the moon, like the sun. There are three rings on the pillow, a moon and two suns: a mother and two fathers. The rings are intertwined.

The thick cloud of incense in church makes it hard to see. The aroma of sagebrush makes me sleepy. I rest my head on the satin pillow, dreaming inside my dream about my new life, a life with two papas.

Emerging from the cloud of smoke, they ride towards me on horseback instead of on their Harleys. They ride the Appaloosas we used to have. I remember their names: Ferdinand and Cornflower, the names my papas gave them when I was just a boy.

NEVER TOO OLD, NEVER TOO LATE

I am happy to have the company of Phaedre, my neighbor, on the long subway ride to and from the farmers' market down on Union Square. She is also my friend, a red-haired young woman from Ireland. I'm a gray-haired old *babushka* from what was once Russia and then became the Soviet Union and now is Russia again. I lived through it all.

My family and I—my brother Nikolai, my daughter Moosha, and my grandchildren Maxim and Nina—arrived in New York after the collapse of the USSR six years ago. I'd dreamed of coming to America my entire life. I'm glad I learned patience as a child. I am now eighty-two years old and still in no hurry. My friend is also patient. I get along with her better than my own daughter, though Phaedre is closer in age to my granddaughter.

Phaedre and I do not attempt to be heard above the screeching and whooshing of the A train when it goes express after leaving our neighborhood in Washington Heights. We do not talk again until it reaches Harlem at 125th Street.

"My grandson speaks of you often, Phaedre. I believe he is falling down for you."

"The expression is just plain old *falling for someone*, Ana," she tells me, smiling. "I would not complain if he has fallen for me. Did you by any chance cast a spell on him?"

"Not a very strong one, my child, more like steering something rather than pushing it along. My recipes are gentle. I try to be kind."

"I understand, Ana," she says. "I just want to be sure his falling for me is Maxim's idea."

"It is certainly Max's idea, dear. But he hesitates. He wastes time. He can't decide. I'm not so much putting a spell on him as I am dispelling the fog he finds himself in."

An old fellow comes up to me and Phaedre, weaving and bobbing as the train lurches. He holds out his hand and I put the coins from my pocket in his dirty palm. He looks down at me and thanks me, offering me God's blessing.

"Thank you," I tell him. "I need all the help I can get."

Phaedre and I emerge from the *Metró*, the subway, at Union Square and Sixteenth Street. The market is crowded today, despite the cold and the snow earlier in the week. It is the last Friday market before Christmas. It is Christmas Eve. Phaedre takes my elbow so we do not get separated.

My eyes twirl inside my head there is so much to see. My nose twitches, inhaling all the aromas: bread and cookies, soup and coffee and tea, and the enormous potted pine trees encircling the park. My ears tingle, too, taking in the tinkling bells, the Christmas music over the loudspeakers, and the chatter of passing conversations in more languages than even I understand.

Faces are rosy and smiling; vendors are eager to please their customers. We stop at Mr. Arkady's poultry stall. He winks at us.

"Pretty fresh today," he says. "And I don't need ice."

"Do you have any live hens today?" I ask him.

"No, Miss Ana. The health department said it wasn't allowed, that chickens are dirty birds. So, I asked him, what about pigeons? Are the pigeons so clean? I don't see you chasing down pigeons. He had no answer for that."

"Well, then, two dead hens, Mr. Arkady," I tell him. "Perhaps there will be less fuss if I do not bring a live chicken on the subway train."

Phaedre laughs.

"It caused quite a commotion when it got loose, Mr. Arkady," she tells him. "Perhaps you wouldn't mind keeping our parcels until we head home. We have other shopping to do."

"Certainly," he tells my friend, handing her our receipts.

We walk on. I have to be careful. There are many icy spots. Phaedre gives me her arm.

Pine trees in their burlap-covered root-balls encircle most of the square. They are decorated for Christmas with multi-colored ornaments and tiny white lights. The trees blot out most of the buildings surrounding Union Square, making it seem that I am once more back at the winter market in Odessa.

I stand still. Phaedre stops beside me. I close my eyes a moment.

The fragrance of the pine trees transports me back to Russia. I am a young girl again, during the Great War in Europe and before the Revolution. My older brother, Nikolai, says something to me, but my mind has been wandering. I open my eyes again.

Nikolai and I stand in the middle of the Odessa market. It is cold and the snow is piled up. There are very few merchants or customers.

"Could you listen to me for once, Ana.," my brother says. "Our neighbors say it was definitely a police wagon that took mother and father away. I went to the local constabulary, but they will tell me nothing. They laughed at me, called me a disloyal son to lose track of my parents. They are the sort of imbecilic bureaucrats that will have no place after the Revolution."

I don't know what more to suggest to Nikolai. We have tried everything we know how to do to locate our parents. We pawned one of our mother's amber bracelets to bribe a guard at the local prison. He took the bribe but failed to deliver any information on Catherine and Leon Mendeleyev. He, too, heaped derisive laughter on our heads. Nikolai said the guard was the sort of dishonest official that will be lined up before a firing squad once the Revolution does away with corruption.

Nikolai has gone from banishing those he dislikes to executing them within the course of a single conversation. Though I am only eight years old, I do not understand how the Revolution will be an improvement on anything.

"Ana, Ana," a voice says, startling me. "Are you all right?"

I know the voice. Someone tugs at my coat sleeve. I open

my eyes. I am back in Union Square. It is my friend, Phaedre.

"Sorry, dear," I tell her. "Sometimes I weave in and out, back and forth, between here and there."

"Where is there, Ana?"

"The Old Country," I tell her. "My parents' house in Odessa. I remember them always at Christmas. The smell of pine boughs takes me back there."

"That is so sweet," Phaedre remarks.

"I am afraid my other association with Christmas, dear child, is that my parents were arrested by the Tsar's police just before Christmas in 1916, over seventy years ago. I have not seen them since."

"Oh, I am so sorry for you, Ana."

"That is how life works, child. There's always a bit of sorrow in our happiness, and a speck of joy in our sadness. Come. We'll stay warmer if we keep moving."

Phaedre takes hold of my elbow again even though this section of the walkway, receiving all of the afternoon sun, is ice-free.

"Oh, do you smell that, Phaedre? It makes my mouth water. The baker must have just taken something out of his little electric oven. Let's go see."

We hurry over to Hoffman's Fine Baked Goods. This time he has set up next to the tea and coffee vendor—a fine idea.

"There you are, Ana," Hoffman tells me. "I expected you 'round about now. I just took your special order out of the oven."

"Phaedre, dear, please do not look. One of the items is for you. We'll go next door and order our tea, Mr. Hoffman. When my items are cool, you may wrap them up individually. Don't forget to mark the names on them."

"I won't, Ana. Is there anything you ladies would like to have with your tea when you return?"

"How about two crescent rolls, Mr. Hoffman. Is that all right with you, Phaedre?"

My friend agrees. Hoffman places our croissants inside his little oven to warm them up. When we return with our paper cups of tea, the pastries are hot enough to melt butter. I pay him for our rolls and for my custom order. I hand one of the oddly-shaped little parcels, wrapped in white paper, to Phaedre.

"What's this?" she asks.

"It's your Christmas present a day early, child."

"But it says 'Maxim' on it."

"Yes, I know, dear. He'll get the one marked 'Phaedre.'"

"Oh, look," she declares. "You've got ones for my cousin, Fitzgerald, and his partner, Antonio, too. How sweet of you, Ana. Isn't there one for Nina?"

"No, she's not yet old enough to have someone special in her life. My granddaughter will receive something else, something just for her."

"You've intrigued me, Ana," Phaedre says. "May I peek at my present?"

Hoffman stands at the counter, waiting to see my neighbor's reaction.

"You may take a peek, Phaedre," I tell her, "but you may not eat the cookie until tomorrow. It has to be eaten on Christmas Day. They are magic cookies."

"Oh, my God. Ana. Mr. Hoffman. It is gorgeous. I couldn't possibly eat a gingerbread cookie that looks like Max. It's exactly how he combs his hair and how he wears his glasses: a little bit crooked. I will save it and put him on the Christmas tree—when we get one, that is."

"You mustn't save the cookie, Phaedre. You and Max must eat each other up. Mr. Hoffman has baked them according to my exact recipe and instructions."

"Of course, Ana, I will do as you say," Phaedre tells me, smiling as one humors an old woman, an eccentric old woman.

She accepts the small brown paper shopping bag from Hoffman containing the other three gingerbread cookies. I don't know whether Hoffman believes they are magic cookies, either, but he has never skimped on the ingredients or failed to follow my recipes to the letter.

"All right, Phaedre," I tell my grandson's girlfriend. "Time to put Max back in his paper. You must not let him see it and, even if he wants to show you his cookie of you, you must not look. You must simply gobble each other up."

"Does that go for my cousin Fitz and his boyfriend Antonio, too?" she asks.

"Yes, child. Love is love."

Phaedre wraps my "grandson" back in his paper and places him inside the brown bag.

"Good-bye, Mr. Hoffman," I tell him. "Thank you. And Happy Chanukah."

"And a Merry Christmas to you and your friend."

I nod to him and continue down the path with Phaedre. When we have finished our tea, she offers to discard our paper cups in the trash.

"No, dear. I have a use for them."

She watches me intently. Removing my mitten, I scoop dirt from one of the potted pine trees into each of the cups. Then I pinch off a tiny bud-bearing branch and use it to poke a hole in the plastic lid. I push the little cutting deep into the dirt.

"One for you and Max, one for Fitzgerald and Antonio."

"Thank you, Ana."

Phaedre puts the coffee cups containing the tiny pine cuttings into the little shopping bag with the cookies. She is a good-hearted neighbor and friend. I am happy she and my grandson have found each other. I believe they will make each other happy for the rest of their lives.

The sun is setting at the end of the long canyon of Fifteenth Street. All the buildings look like reddish stone, like the sandstone buildings in Odessa.

"I'm looking for the fellow who sells candy, Phaedre. Have you seen him? I'm looking for the little white candy beads they sprinkle on nonpareils."

"I haven't seen him yet, Ana, but we haven't been down this path," she tells me, pointing.

The air grows chillier even though the sunset has suffused it with a warm, rosy glow.

"There he is," she says. "Be careful of this icy patch."

Mr. Collins has decorated his stall with a festive Yuletide banner and two enormous striped candy-canes.

"My dear, Ana," he says to me. "It is always nice to see you.

Merry Christmas."

"Likewise, Mr. Collins. I am looking for the tiny sugar beads they sprinkle on chocolate nonpareils. Just the beads, if you please."

"Hmm," he says, stroking his gray beard.

Collins nods to Phaedre as he takes a plastic box from beneath the counter of his stall. The box contains many little drawers. He opens several before finding what he wants.

"Here we are," he tells me. "The package is opened. This is all I have left. Excuse me a moment."

The candyman waits on a customer interested in bark candy and a box of hand-dipped chocolates. He takes her money and packs up her purchase.

"Now," he says, returning to me and holding up the opened cellophane bag of white sugary beads.

"That will do just fine, Mr. Collins. What do I owe you for the candy beads?" I ask him.

"It's too small an amount to charge you, Ana. Merry Christmas."

"Same to you, Mr. Collins. Thank you."

Phaedre and I find a bench from which most of the snow has been brushed off. We sit down and I pull off my mittens. I take the bag of sugar beads from my pocket and, reaching over, sprinkle them into the shopping bag my friend has placed on the ground between us. She looks at me questioningly.

"Tiny ornaments for the tiny trees," I tell her.

"Of course," she says, laughing. "You are so inventive, Ana. You seem to really enjoy Christmas."

"Yes, very much. It has always been my favorite time of the year, despite many unpleasant memories that got tacked onto the holiday."

Phaedre looks down into the bag.

"The sugar beads have all stuck to the pine needles, Ana. They look like tiny Christmas ornaments."

"I was hoping they would," I tell her. "My parents preferred simple decorations for our Christmas trees."

"Were you ever able to find out what happened to them, Ana?"

"The Ministry of Prisons told me that, as my parents and other prisoners were being transported to Irkutsk in Siberia, the train was derailed by members of the Revolutionary Guard. Most of the passengers were killed. My parents' bodies were never recovered."

"Oh, how terrible," my friend tells me.

"Not at all," I reply. "You have to understand Russian bureaucratese. It can be taken whatever way you please. I took it to mean that their bodies were never recovered because they had escaped. I am hopeful my parents and I will meet again before I am gone. That is my Christmas wish this year, as it has been every year since my parents disappeared."

"But how old would they be?" Phaedre asks, helping me up from the park bench.

I take her hand, squinting my eyes to do a bit of calculation.

"They'd be a hundred-and-two, dear. Certainly not too old. It's quite possible this is the year I shall see them one last time."

Phaedre squeezes my hand. It comforts me. She is such a kind person. My grandson is very lucky. Phaedre and I start walking.

"Oh, there," I say. "The fabric remnants. I see something for my daughter, Moosha. The brocaded sofa pillows. Would you be able to carry them home?"

"Yes, of course," she replies.

We approach Mr. Finkelstein. He remembers me.

"Happy Christmas, Miss Ana. What has caught your eye?"

"The white pillows," I tell him. "The ones with the gold tassels."

"Those are the only pillows I have today."

"Then they shall have to do," I remark.

We chuckle. Phaedre joins in.

"And for you, Ana, a special price in honor of Christmas and Chanukah," Finkelstein says.

He figures on a small pad of paper. He does more calculating than was involved in Mr. Einstein's equations. He quotes me a price and I wrinkle my nose.

"Look, Miss Ana. I don't want to pack them up and take

them home again. Make me a reasonable offer and they are yours."

"Of course it will be a reasonable offer, Mr. Finkelstein. I wouldn't waste your time with an unreasonable offer, would I? Five dollars for the pair."

"All right. All right," Finkelstein says, holding up his palms. "But only because it is Christmas and Chanukah and it is late in the day—and because I like you."

"Deal," I tell him, counting out the money from my change purse.

Finkelstein pushes the pillows into an oversized plastic bag, the kind that fits in a trash can. He draws the strings and hands the bag to Phaedre. I take the paper bag containing the pine cuttings and the gingerbread cookies from her. We wish Finkelstein a Merry Christmas and he wishes us a Happy Chanukah.

"Yes, dear," I tell Phaedre. "I know what you are thinking. They are the ugliest sofa pillows in all of creation. Moosha will love them."

She laughs. I put the paper shopping bag in my right hand. Phaedre slings the plastic bag with the throw pillows over her shoulder like Father Frost with his sack of presents. She latches onto my left arm.

"Only two more items," I tell her. "Something for my brother and a gift for Nina. I think she would like a piece of jewelry. I wonder if Mr. Ordoubadi is here today. It's getting late."

"And snowing again," Phaedre remarks. "We have not gone this way," she suggests.

Ordoubadi's booth is at the end of the walk near the Park Avenue side of Union Square. His banner announces "Fine Jewelry from Around the World," listing all seven continents and the nine planets below that. He has a handmade sign wishing Happy Kwanza.

Ordoubadi is not behind the counter of his stall. Instead, there is an old couple in their hooded winter coats, shawls, and knit caps, slouched forward in their lawn chairs, snoring. As one breathes in, the other breathes out, making their gentle racket continuous.

Not wishing to disturb them, Phaedre and I examine the

jewelry on their black velvet trays on the counter. The snowflakes land on the velvet, pausing a moment before vanishing. Phaedre points to a small but flashy bracelet made of what appears to be polished amber. My mother had a similar piece on her wrist when the Tsar's police clamped manacles on her.

A strange swirl of heavy snow descends out of nowhere, making it hard to see. The old couple stirs and, stooped over, come to the counter. All I can see are their eyes, noses, and smiling mouths—no foreheads or chins. The snow stops abruptly.

"May we help you, young lady," the old woman asks, grinning.

I think she is talking to Phaedre, but they look straight at me. I laugh.

"Yes, we mean you, Ana," the old man says.

They pull back their fur-fringed hoods and remove their knit caps. Though there are many layers of wrinkles and furrows, I recognize them by their dazzling blue eyes.

"Mother. Father," I say, the words catching in my throat. My heart races and I feel dizzy.

I drop my shopping bag. Phaedre leans the bag of pillows against the counter and puts her arm around me, steadying me. I cannot see for the tears filling my eyes, nor speak for choking on the words.

My parents' smiles tell me all I wish to know. They converse with me in Russian.

"Yes, daughter, it has been a long time of many winters and many hardships. We are here in answer to your Christmas wish. Merry Christmas, Ana."

My parents come from behind the counter and wrap their arms around me, encircling me with hugs and warmth. They are much shorter than I remember. We cry tears of sorrow and weep for joy.

I show them I still carry my lucky rabbit's foot from my girlhood.

"I never lost hope," I say.

"Nor did we, child. Please introduce us to your friend, Ana," my father says in English. His voice is still strong, but the cold has made it brittle.

"This is my friend and neighbor, Phaedre McGuirk. She will soon be engaged to marry your great-grandson Maxim Andreyevich."

"I believe Max has to propose to me first, Ana," Phaedre says, chuckling.

"Oh, he will do so quite soon, child," I assure her. "Perhaps as early as tomorrow."

"Are you both really here?" Phaedre asks my mother and father. "Or has your daughter put a spell on me?"

"We are mostly here," my father tells her. "A little less than most people, but quite a bit more than some."

"I see," she replies, though I doubt she does.

"We will have to return home soon, Ana. Were you interested in my polished amber bracelet, dear?" my mother asks me.

"Yes, Mama. I remember it fondly. I'd like your great-granddaughter, Nina, to have it. I recognized the bracelet before I recognized you."

"It has changed less," she says, smiling a beautiful, shining, happy smile. "You may have it, Ana. We have no need of money. Take darling Nina our blessings."

"I will," I promise.

My mother places her amber bracelet and the matching amber ring in a tiny muslin bag and ties the drawstring. I accept it from her with a deep bow.

"We have a letter for Nikolai. Please give it to him with our love, Ana," my father says.

"Yes, Papa, I will. Thank you. I know my brother will not believe I have spoken with you, even with my neighbor as witness."

I put the tiny cloth bag of jewelry and the letter for Nikolai in my coat pocket.

"We must go, dear Ana. We are so very tired," my mother says.

"It is quite exhausting standing in two places at once," my father adds.

My parents kiss me on both cheeks and I return their

embraces. Our cheeks are salty with tears. They touch Phaedre's hand, but she does not seem to feel it. They grow thin, wispy, like the steam of our breath disappearing into the frigid air.

My friend stands with her mouth agape, her eyes wide.

"They just vanished," she says, her voice quivering. "Like mist."

"Yes, I know, child. The magic recipe that brought my mother and father here works for only a short time. My heart is glad. I am grateful I saw them one more time before they left this world."

"But it's very startling to someone who doesn't believe in magic," Phaedre says.

"Perhaps now you believe a little bit more?"

"Yes, but I'm still confused."

"Confusion is a condition of life, child, with or without magic," I tell her. She smiles and takes my hand.

"Come," I tell her. "We still have to stop by Mr. Arkady to pick up our chickens. It is getting late. Our families will be eager to see us."

The butcher hands Phaedre the paper shopping bag containing our chickens. He has wrapped cardboard around the handles to make it easier for her to carry. She slings the plastic bag with the ugly pillows over her other shoulder and takes the drawstrings.

I carry the bag with the gingerbread cookies and miniature Christmas trees, taking hold of Phaedre's elbow with my left hand. We walk to the *Metró* station at Fourteenth Street. We take the handicapped elevator at street level down to the subway platform. We must ride the L train over to Eighth Avenue to catch the A train. We carry on our conversation between the racket of arriving and departing trains.

"Since you and Max will be having supper with Fitzgerald and Antonio tomorrow at your apartment, I shall leave all four of the gingerbread cookies with you, my dear. I'll explain what each of you must do. You must not get it wrong or the magic in the cookies will not work."

"I shall pay close attention, Ana. I promise."

"God bless you, child," I tell her. "I shall explain how to care for the baby Christmas trees, too. I hope that the other little gift I have for you will come in handy—just in case," I say, patting her hand.

———————◦◦———————

When her cousin Fitz and his companion, Antonio, leave Phaedre's basement apartment on Ft. Washington Avenue, she and Maxim kiss each other with a bit more passion than they felt comfortable expressing in front of their friends.

"That was a fine Christmas supper, Phaedre," Max tells her, kissing her again.

"Don't forget the food Fitz and Antonio brought."

"Believe me, I haven't. Their *chile rellenos* were incredibly tasty, but a bit too spicy for my Russian tongue."

"You'll get used to it, Max. New York comes in so many flavors. What do you say we get the clean-up out of the way? I can't wait to open the magic cookie from your grandma."

"I'm sorry you've had to listen to her nonsense, Phaedre. It's not enough she bothers her family with her magic formulas."

He puts the bones of the chicken carcass in the garbage can beneath the sink. They are picked clean.

"I love your grandma, Max. It's not nonsense. I'm not sure I believe it as fervently as she does, but there is something going on with her recipes I can't explain. Didn't the full-size Christmas tree growing out of the paper coffee cup convince you?"

Max shrugs.

"A clever trick, I'll admit," he says, "but it's not magic. There's no such thing."

Phaedre fills the greasy roasting pan with hot water and detergent and sets it aside. Filling one side of the sink with water and soap, she washes the bowls and dishes and silverware. There are no leftovers.

Phaedre hands the washed dishes over to Max who rinses them in the other side of the sink, stacking them in the drainer atop the counter in the tiny kitchen.

When they have finished, Max wraps his arms around

Phaedre's waist and kisses her neck. He makes it clear what he'd prefer to be doing. Phaedre reaches for the wrapped Christmas cookies on the dining table.

"I can't believe we're going through with this," Max tells her.

"Yes, we are, Max. And you're going to follow your grandma's instructions to the letter or you can forget about sex until next Christmas when you'll have another chance to redeem yourself. Do you want to open yours here or in the bedroom?"

"I'll stay here. You take the bedroom, Phaedre."

"All right. And no cheating. No peeking."

Phaedre and Max unwrap their custom gingerbread cookies from Mr. Hoffman. They smile at the same instant and have nearly the same thought.

That looks too much like Phaedre. I couldn't possibly bite into it.

That looks so much like Max. How could I possibly devour him?

But neither wishes to be the one to break the spell of Grandma's magic recipe.

Phaedre gnaws first at Max's feet, moving up to the knees and thighs, giving a little chuckle when she devours his privates. She saves the head for last. It is the part of the caricature in sugar frosting that most resembles him. She pops it in her mouth, but it is too big to swallow whole.

Closing her eyes, she bites down on Max's head, grinding it to bits. It is the sweetest part of the cookie with the most sugar frosting on it. She smiles to herself.

"There. I've done it. You're inside me now, Max. I've gobbled you up, my love."

She lays back on her pillow, looking up at the pattern of steam pipes and their shadows on the ceiling. She realizes she is horny and hopes Max hurries up with his cookie.

Max first bites off Phaedre's head, finding the cookie a bit too sweet. He manages to swallow her head whole. Now the cookie no longer resembles anyone, especially not someone he loves.

Max licks the cookie woman's breasts, her belly button,

and her vagina until all the frosting has melted into his mouth and only the gingerbread remains. Thinking of Phaedre, he nibbles the gingerbread until it is gone.

"Now you're part of me, my love. I've eaten you all up."

He thinks it was a pretty good cookie, possibly made with real ginger. He wonders if Phaedre has finished her cookie of him and knocks on the bedroom door.

"Are you finished with me, Phaedre?" he asks. "May I come in?"

She chuckles at his wordplay. "Please. I've been waiting for you."

Max finds her stripped naked, propped against many pillows, her legs in a pose he can only think of as seductive—except he's not thinking at all. His single-mindedness crowds out all thought.

Taking off his clothes while walking towards the bed, he gets tangled up and nearly topples on top of Phaedre.

"I'm glad you are so eager," she tells him. "Enthusiasm goes a long way with me."

His undershorts get snagged on his erection. Phaedre helps extricate him. They both laugh.

Phaedre and Max tell themselves they want to go slow so their love-making lasts, but they've been ready to jump on each other since their supper guests left. They were quite prepared to do it right on the dining room floor, the last course of their supper—dessert.

Phaedre straddles Max's stomach. She lowers herself slowly onto his erection, her breasts jiggling happily as she bounces up and down on her knees. They moan in unison.

The brevity of their love-making is outshone by its intensity. They collapse on their sides, theirs arms wrapped around each other, their legs entwined, breathing heavily.

"I've just had a crazy thought," Max says, propping himself up on one elbow. "I was just wondering. Will you marry me, Phaedre?"

"Oh, my God. Yes, Max. Of course I will marry you. I love you."

"I'm afraid I don't yet have an engagement ring, Phaedre. The idea to propose only just occurred to me."

"It's the sentiment that counts," she tells him.

"Oh, good. That's going to save me a lot of money."

She tickles his ribs. They lie down beside one another and get beneath the covers again.

"Max," she says. "I received this ring of polished amber from your grandmother yesterday, just in case you decided to pop the question."

"Just in case, huh?" he says.

"Well, she was right, wasn't she, Max? The ring belonged to your great-grandmother."

She places the small but heavy ring in his palm. It catches a glint from the bedside lamp.

Max takes up Phaedre's hand and places the ring on her finger. They smile and kiss each other with many long, slow kisses, only coming up now and then for air.

Phaedre admires the ring by the light of her bedside lamp. Then she turns the lamp down, and she and Max snuggle against each other. By the light of the streetlamps, they see it is snowing.

They spend the rest of Christmas telling each other the oldest and most outrageous stories they recall about their families. Now and then, Pharedre takes her hand from beneath the covers to look at her ring of amber.

It is the best Christmas either of them remembers.

———————◦◦———————

Fitzgerald and Antonio rush inside their apartment across from Van Cortlandt Park in The Bronx. It was a cold and windy walk from the last stop on the 1 train at 242nd Street. They have only been sharing the one-bedroom apartment for a month.

They hold each other and kiss.

"That's the best way to warm up that I know of," Fitz tells his friend.

Antonio bends over to turn on the lights on their Christmas tree, the one grown from a seedling in a carry-out coffee cup. The little sprout was given to them by Madame Ana, their friend

Max's grandmother. Her instructions had been simply to give it a little water and to think good thoughts.

Fitz grabs Antonio's rear end as he fishes for something else beneath their tree.

"Careful," Antonio warns his buddy. "If you're naughty, Santa's not going to come."

"I'm not being naughty. I'm being nice. Besides, I think Santa's already been here."

Antonio stands up and hands Fitz a package wrapped in brown paper and tied with white string. They smile.

"Just a minute," Fitz says.

He retrieves a similarly wrapped package—also tied with white string—from beneath their bed. He hands the parcel to Antonio. They both laugh. Antonio unties the white string on his present.

"Maybe we should eat Madame Ana's Christmas cookies first," Fitz suggests. "Do you want to stay here in the living room or move to the bedroom?"

"I'll go in the bedroom," Antonio replies. "We'll open our other presents out here later, OK?"

"Sure," Fitz tells him. "I can't imagine what you've gotten me," he says, winking.

When Fitz hears Antonio close the bedroom door, he unwraps the cookie from its white paper. It is a sort of caricature, a cartoon version of Antonio rendered in frosting, wearing blue jeans, leather jacket, and biker boots. The face looks exactly like his buddy with its deep brown eyes and glistening black hair.

Fitz licks off Antonio's Levi's and boots, getting a little bit hard as he does so. He laps at the leather jacket until Antonio is naked, the hue of his skin the warm color of the gingerbread. Eating Antonio's brown cookie body, Fitz saves his head for last.

"Thank you, Madame Ana," he says. "Maybe it wasn't your intention, but that cookie has gotten me very randy."

In their bedroom, Antonio takes his cookie out of its paper. He laughs, thinking how much fun it will be to gobble his friend up. He breaks the gingerbread cookie in half and bites off Fitz's head. Then he devours his leather jacket. The frosting is too sweet but the cookie is good.

Antonio finishes eating Fitz's leather jacket and starts chewing on his boots and Levi's. He finds himself getting aroused.

"What a fun present," he says to himself. "Thank you, Madame Ana."

Antonio opens the bedroom door a crack and hollers out.

"Are you finished yet, buddy?" he asks.

"Yeah, I am," Fitz replies. "I've gobbled you all up."

Antonio joins Fitz in the living room. They sit on their slightly sagging secondhand sofa, admiring their Christmas tree. They hand each other their presents and kiss each other.

"Happy Christmas," Fitz tells his friend.

"Feliz Navidad," Antonio replies.

After removing the string and brown paper from their presents, they laugh heartily. As they suspected, they'd each gotten the other a pair of shrink-to-fit Levi's. The fact that they wear the same size only makes it more hilarious.

Antonio brings a bottle of tequila from the kitchen and two small glasses. Fitz retrieves his bottle of Old Curmudgeon whisky. They each enjoy one shot each of whisky and tequila. They feel quite feliz and happy.

Fitz places his hand on Antonio's thigh. Their blue jeans reveal growing boners.

"Want to break in our new Levi's?" Fitz suggests.

"Tonight?"

"Yeah, why not? It's still early," Fitz replies. "We're both plenty randy, thanks to those love-potion cookies."

"But how will we get dry?" Antonio asks.

"The landlord's pumping out plenty of heat tonight. We'll stay in the bathroom next to the riser pipes. We'll be dry in no time."

"OK, buddy," Antonio says. "It'll be fun. We haven't baptized new Levi's together in a while."

They lead each other by the hand to the bedroom where they strip down to their skin and put on their new, stiff, shrink-to-fit blue jeans.

Antonio and Fitz head to the bathroom. They close the

door and fill the old claw-foot tub with hot water. In no time, it feels like a sauna.

With Fitz at the front of the tub and Antonio behind him, they slip down into the hot water, sucking in their breath. As the heavy denim begins to shrink on their bodies, the outline of their boners becomes clear. Antonio nudges closer to his partner and puts his arms around him. The water in the tub looks like a vat of bluing.

"Oh, this feels so good after our walk home in the cold," Fitz tells him.

"I hope it's going to feel even better," Antonio remarks as he strokes Fitz's boner through the crotch of his wet Levi's.

As Antonio rubs his own hard-on against Fitz's backside, they move closer to the edge of climax. Fitz makes deep purring noises. They try to slow down but are too eager.

Since Antonio is in charge of both their erections, it is not surprising that they cream their jeans at the same instant. He feels Fitz's throbbing boner as they both shudder. Antonio leans back in the tub and Fitz lies back against his chest. They shut their eyes and enjoy all the sensations their wet lovemaking has brought them.

When the water has grown merely warm, Fitz pulls out the stopper and drains the tub. The porcelain is stained blue by the indigo dye in their jeans.

They sit on the edge of the tub, Antonio at the back, Fitz in the front, letting most of the water and indigo drip from their Levi's and stream down the drain.

The two friends take turns either standing in front of the heat riser pipes or sitting opposite them on the lid of the commode, relishing the feeling of the drying denim shrinking up on their bodies.

They spend the rest of Christmas telling each other the oldest and most outrageous stories they recall about their families. It is the best Christmas either of them remembers.

I stand at the kitchen window watching curtains of snow swirl around the towers of the George Washington Bridge. The rest of the family has gone to bed.

My daughter Moosha loved the ugly brocaded sofa cushions. Nina shrieked with delight over the polished amber bracelet. She loved it even more when she learned it had come from her great-grandparents.

I hope my simple recipes have brought happiness to the two young couples by helping them realize the depth of their love.

I brew a pot of tea and sit at the kitchen table. It is 11:30, only a half-hour of Christmas left to enjoy.

A rap at the kitchen window startles me. Nikolai has again climbed to our sixth-floor apartment via the fire escape.

My brother drives a rented limousine. He works on Christmas and other holidays to make extra money and earn generous tips.

Nikolai uses the fire escape because he does not like people in the hallways and on the elevator watching where he goes. No doubt it is a leftover fear from his years of being under the scrutiny of nosy neighbors back in Russia. They regularly reported his strange habits to the police as though strangeness were itself a crime.

"I am happy you made it, Nikolai," I tell him. "Merry Christmas."

"Merry Christmas, Ana," he says, kissing my cheeks. His cheeks are cold.

I pour hot tea into our glasses and add two sugar-cubes to each. I fetch the bottle of Lantern Fuel vodka from the pantry and pour two healthy splashes into our glasses.

"Za zdaróvye," we toast each other

My brother takes a thick envelope from his uniform jacket and hands it to me.

"I have given a little trinket to Nina that she will forget by next Christmas," he says. "But this is my overtime and tip money for her art school. She will be a great artist some day."

"Bless you, Nikolai. Moosha and I wondered how we could afford her art school. There is something that came for you, too,"

I tell him, withdrawing the envelope from our parents from my apron pocket and handing it to him.

He glances at it and then looks at me. I would not be surprised that he recognizes our mother's beautiful script, even after the passage of so many years. After breaking the seal, he opens the flap and takes out the letter. He unfolds it and takes his spectacles from his inside jacket pocket.

I watch my brother's face as he reads, noting the crisscross of lines and wrinkles, furrows and scars inscribed there. Two World Wars and the Revolution and the countless purges through which he passed have written their history on his flesh.

Nikolai re-folds the letter from our parents and places his hands over it. He trembles and shakes as though grappling with a powerful force. He stares at me, pleading in his sparkling blue eyes.

Tears well up. Only the dam of his will holds them back.

At last they burst forth, a tiny stream that becomes a torrent. His chest heaves and he leans forward, holding his head in his hands. Taking the handkerchief from his chauffeur's jacket, he sobs until my own heart is on the verge of breaking.

I get up and stand behind my brother, rubbing his shoulders and stroking his neck.

"Nikolai," I tell him. "Let it go. Let it all go."

His sobbing subsides. He dries his eyes and blows into his handkerchief. Sighing, he takes a few deep breaths and smiles up at me.

"I don't know whether your magic is anything more than trickery, my dear Ana. I have wanted to cry for over sixty years, but there were no tears left after our parents were arrested and taken away. Bless you, my sister. I have at last been washed and forgiven for all I have done."

I pour only a little vodka into our glasses and go back to my chair. Nikolai toasts to our health. He takes my hand and squeezes it.

"This is the best Christmas I remember, Ana. Not since I was twelve years old have I felt thrilled to be alive."

"Yes, me too, Nikolai. God has blessed us all with love and

kindness."

His tears have refreshed my brother, washed him, made him as clean as the snow falling on the rungs and railings of the fire escape outside the kitchen window.

We tell each other our memories of the old family home in Odessa, shedding more tears, but also enjoying laughter until our sides ache.

Nikolai does not return to work this Christmas. There is enough money for Nina's art school. We talk at the kitchen table and drink tea—with just a little vodka—until the sun comes up and all the shadows melt away.

About the Author

Brian Allan Skinner has written and published more than 120 short stories which have appeared in small press and literary magazines, as well as anthologies, in the United States, Canada, and Ireland.

He is a former poetry and non-fiction reviewer for *Kirkus Reviews* and a production artist for *Scientific American Newsletters* in New York City.

In 2015, Brian moved to Taos, New Mexico, which he first visited with his grandmother on a cross-country train trip aboard the Santa Fe Chief in 1960. He quickly settled into the thriving artistic and literary communities of Taos where he draws sustenance and inspiration from his many artist and writer friends.